I0417875

MR. JONES & ME

LINDSAY MARIE MILLER

MR. JONES & ME. Copyright © 2016 by Lindsay Marie Miller.

Cover Photo by Volodymyr Tverdokhlib/Shutterstock

All rights reserved. No part of this book may be reproduced or transmitted in any form without written permission of the author, except by a reviewer who may quote brief passages for review purposes only.

This is a work of fiction. Names, characters, places, and incidents are the product of the author's imagination or are used fictitiously. Any resemblance to actual persons, living or dead, events, or locales is purely coincidental.

For more info, please visit www.lindsaymariemillerauthor.com

Praise for *ME & MR. JONES*

"A Suspenseful, Fast Paced and Utterly Brilliant Read!"

—*Amazon Reviewer*

"Left me with a massive book hangover!"

— *A Book Lover's Emporium*

"A fast paced, quick read that will hook you on this series."

—*A One-Click Addict's Book Blog*

"Not your typical forbidden fruit story."

—*Amazon Reviewer*

"...totally blew my mind."

—*Kylie's Fiction Addiction*

"Hot, sexy... Loved it."

—*Amazon Reviewer*

DON'T MISS THESE OTHER BOOKS BY
LINDSAY MARIE MILLER

The Girl in the Woods

Emerald Green

Honey Gold

Me & Mr. Jones

Jungle Eyes

Island Smile

Coastal Spirit

Single

An Arrangement

An Accident

Mercy

AND LOOK FOR HER NEW NOVEL

Available in January 2018

And I saw a new heaven and a new earth: for the first heaven and the first earth were passed away; and there was no more sea.

Revelation 21:1

Part I
The Golden Girl

Chapter 1

A cool breeze swept through the moonlit parking lot and I shivered. Jeremy walked me to my car, his ginger locks glinting in hues of orange and gold beneath the street lamps. For a Friday night, the restaurant had proved worthy, pulling in a fair amount of guests eager to be served. We had closed the place down together, a near-nightly ritual for the two of us. But now that the clock was just shy of striking eleven, the only place I wanted to be was home.

Yawning, I followed the subtle glow of Jeremy's taillights on the road, my eyes drifting to the rearview mirror every so often. When we parted ways at a fork dividing town from the outskirts surrounding it, I felt the full weight of exhaustion set in. It had been a rough first semester of graduate school, and the impending Winter Break couldn't arrive fast enough.

Alone on a deserted highway, I had the uncanny sensation that someone was watching me. Ever since last summer, it was a feeling I could not shake. The feeling of a voyeur lurking in the shadows with a camera aimed and ready.

Once I reached the turn to our house, I shifted the car into a lower gear and soared up the steep drive, sheltered beneath the canopy that only tall trees could provide. When I parked in front of the humble abode and got out, my back ached from standing on my feet all week, both day and night. I lugged my bag full of books up the steps and dragged my feet across the wooden boards of the porch. By the time I let myself in the house and closed the door behind me, relief filled my lungs, and I exhaled with pleasure.

Careful not to wake Cabel, I crept up the staircase and entered the master bedroom with the quiet stealth of a jungle cat. He was already asleep in bed, everything but his strong arms resting beneath the covers. As I listened for the sound of his breathing, my heart rate increased until he respired aloud.

Setting my things down on the floor, I slipped into the bathroom and shut the door behind me. Once my shoes were off, I turned the shower on and stripped down until my skin was bare. With my clothes in a nice pile by the door, I stepped into the steaming cascade and pulled the shower curtain back to keep the heat inside.

Letting my hair down, I stood beneath the water as the warm moisture covered my body, relaxing the stiffness and tightening in my shoulders and back. For the month of December, it was predictably frigid, and I had been dreaming of a hot bath or shower all day. Now that one had finally arrived, I couldn't help but tilt my head back and sigh.

As I threaded my fingers through my wet locks, two hands slithered around my waist, and I flinched.

"Sorry," Cabel whispered, his chin on my shoulder as his breath caressed my ear. "I didn't mean to scare you."

Taking a breath of oxygen, I turned into his embrace to find my beautiful golden boy, blonde-haired and blue-eyed. He was just how I had always remembered him in my dreams during those tortuous years that we had spent apart. He was all that I would ever need in a man and more.

"It's okay." My hands slid down the length of his arms, searching and roaming. "I didn't mean to wake you."

Cabel leaned his face against mine and paused just before my mouth. "I don't mind."

I felt my cheeks stain with blush, as he tilted my face up in his hands and gently touched my lips with his. A shiver ran down my spine, electric and enlightening, unlocking every ounce of desire. When the kiss came to an end, I gazed up at him impatiently.

"You look tired," he noted, planting his fingers in my hair.

"Thanks," I coolly remarked, lowering my head.

"Hey." Cabel grasped my chin in the palm of his hand and lifted it up. "I'm just worried about you is all."

"*Worried* about me?"

"Yes," he softly crooned, gliding his thumb along every curve of my face.

"Why?"

Cabel hesitated, his ice blue eyes like glaciers in an arctic sea. When his knuckles brushed across my cheekbone, I parted my lips to breathe. With him around, I always needed more air.

"You're in class all day, working at the restaurant, and then coming home to study all night. It's too much."

"Cabel, I can handle it," I demanded.

"I'm not saying that you can't." He tugged at my elbows and looked away. "But you're making things hard on yourself for no reason."

"Cabel, I have to support myself. Just like any other grad student."

"But your situation is different," he urged. "You have a husband."

My eyes darted up to meet his, as I took a step back and crossed my arms over my chest. Cabel cocked his head to the side and bit the edge of his lip. When he moved towards me, I chewed at the inside of my cheek and stared.

Cabel placed his hands on my shoulders and pressed his forehead to mine. "Let me take care of you," he pleaded.

"Maybe I don't want to be taken care of," I confessed, shaking my head from side to side.

"Baby," he coaxed.

"No." I stood my ground and peered into his eyes. "I have to pay my own way. Grad school is expensive, but with the money I make waiting tables—"

"I know it's expensive," he interrupted. "I've been there."

"Yes, but—"

"Quit your job at the restaurant. Focus on school." His hands smoothed down the sides of my arms. "Focus on me."

Furrowing my brow, I regarded him questionably, unable to understand his meaning.

"I miss you," he said. "Between work and school, there is never any time for us."

I moistened my lips and turned my head, watching the water stream down in rivulets as it ran across my feet. Though I had tried to deny it, I knew my hectic schedule was cutting into time I would rather spend with Cabel. While my life wouldn't always be like this, ignoring the problem was never good for a marriage. Especially one as young as ours.

"I know," I finally admitted. When I looked back at him, tears were welling up in my eyes. "I don't want to lose you."

Cabel took me in his arms and tucked my head beneath his chin. We stood in the shower, my cheek to his chest, just living in the warmth and comfort of each other. There was a certain level of intimacy, a certain degree of trust that we had always been able to maintain. I was more terrified than anything of letting it slip away.

"You're not going to," Cabel insisted. His palm skimmed over my back in a delicate motion, while I clung to his side. "Just promise me you'll think about it."

"I will."

Cabel leaned me back in his arms and grinned. "Okay."

* * *

I woke up late in the night, shivering from head to toe. When I reached for the covers, I discovered that Cabel had pulled them all off me and was presently snuggled beneath them on the other side of the bed. Scowling, I reached for the edge of the outermost layer and yanked. But the weight of Cabel's body kept half of the blanket underneath him. Too tired to play tug-of-war, I shook Cabel's arm, and he stirred awake.

"Cabel," I hissed, still jerking at the blanket. "I'm freezing."

"What?" he grumbled, slowly peeling his eyes open.

"Give me some cover," I commanded, while he unraveled himself from the sheets and blankets.

"Sorry." Cabel tossed my share of the covers over my body, and I curled into a ball beneath them.

Even in the dark, I felt his eyes on me. Resting my head on the pillow, I wrapped my arms around myself to get warm. But then Cabel tangled his legs through mine and his hands were touching my waist. He placed his chin at the crux of my neck and shoulder, as I felt the stubble on his face against my skin.

"Hmm," I hummed, my lips buzzing at the sound.

His fingertips skated over my ribcage, awakening my senses at the most gentle contact. When his mouth touched my neck, I turned over in bed and angled my body towards his. Cabel rubbed his nose against mine, then tucked a fallen lock of hair behind my ear before his knuckles drifted along my clavicle.

When our lips met, I knew that as long as I remained in the strength of Cabel's arms, I would never be cold again.

Chapter 2

Monday afternoon found me buried in research, as I analyzed data regarding psychopathy in the family. Case study after case study detailed accounts of abusive fathers, husbands, murderers, assaulters, rapists. Ever since my father's death, I had been drawn to abnormal psychology, a collection of instances in the mind, when things go wrong. Somehow, knowing that he could never be cured made me want to diagnose and treat his condition all the more. There was a fine line between evil and mental. But I was having a hard time drawing it.

Content with the progress I had made on my thesis today, I packed my bags and headed to Cabel's office. All his talk about the two of us needing to spend more time together was getting to me. While I hadn't decided whether or not I was going to give up waiting tables yet, I had considered making an adjustment or two to my schedule in the New Year. With the semester nearly finished, it hardly seemed feasible to make any drastic changes until January. By then, I could talk to Jeremy about cutting my shifts down to once or twice a week, and that would be compromise enough.

After taking the elevator to the fourth floor, I strolled down the hall until I heard the sound of laughter coming through Cabel's door. It was not my husband's chuckling that caused me alarm, but the feminine giggling that undoubtedly belonged to another woman. Suspicious, I slowed my steps just outside his office, but eavesdropping only proved to be more infuriating.

Tapping my knuckles against the door, I listened for the dissolution of her chatter. But the only sound more distressing than that was the rapid pounding of my pulse and heart.

"Come in," Cabel called.

When I opened the door and stepped inside, it was clear to see that he was not expecting my arrival. Sitting across from him in the chair directly facing his desk, the seat that I had once occupied as a student, was a woman I did not recognize.

"Finley," he hesitated, swallowing. "What are you doing here?"

What a strange reaction. I wasn't aware that it was necessary to schedule an appointment when I held the title of wife and the word Mrs. in front of his surname, which I had recently taken. Perhaps I should have called first.

"I just wanted to stop by before I head to work."

The woman uncrossed her legs and held her hand out. "Hi, I'm Jane."

Flicking my eyes between the woman and Cabel, I took a step towards Jane and shook her hand. In the moment of our first encounter, I noticed a familiarity about the stranger.

Golden blonde hair. Ice blue eyes. Smooth, tan skin, though it was December. Pearly white teeth. Red lips the color of rose petals.

As another woman, she was my worst nightmare. The fact that she was wearing a red dress that hugged every curve of her voluptuous breasts and trim waist didn't help either. There was a string of pearls around her neck, and her left hand looked barren without a ring. Despite their similar features, I had the uncanny feeling that Jane wasn't Cabel's sister.

"Finley, this is Dr. Jane Adams. She'll be teaching social psychology here next semester."

"It's nice to meet you," I offered, fighting every urge to say something else.

Jane parted her lips over her teeth in a disturbing smile. "Charmed."

"Finley is getting her master's degree in abnormal psychology," Cabel went on. "She's nearly done with her first semester."

Jane leaned her elbow against the arm of the chair and grinned up at me. "How are you liking grad school?"

"Oh, it's fine." I shrugged my shoulders and walked around the desk to Cabel.

When he set his hand along the small of my back, I gave him a quick kiss, and he curled his arm around my waist. The look on Jane's face was priceless, as she shut her mouth before I had the chance to count how many seconds she had actually been gaping.

"Finley is my wife," Cabel clarified, as if there was any question about it.

"Oh." She looked stunned, her radiance diminishing. "Well..." Her eyes sank to the floor, before she reluctantly lifted them up to meet mine. "Congratulations then."

"Thank you," I answered.

Cabel merely nodded in her direction.

"I should get going," she suggested, as neither of us disagreed. "I'll see you around, Cabel." Jane stood, and her focus turned to me. "It was nice meeting you."

"You too," I said, ready for her to be gone.

Jane trudged over the threshold, her blood red toenails and matching high heels on full display. But then she turned back into the doorway, and her glassy eyes found Cabel's.

"I guess things really have changed. Haven't they?"

Cabel set his finger on his chin and looked away, eyeing the bookcase against the wall. Melancholy, Jane frowned at him, and then narrowed her eyes at me with a glare. When she continued down the hall and disappeared out of sight, I sauntered across the room and shut the door to Cabel's office. She had failed to close it on her way out.

"What was that about?"

Cabel sighed, and when he furrowed his brow, the lines etched into his forehead worried me. "We went to Cornell together," he confessed.

"Oh." I inched closer to him, nearly sitting down in the chair she had just occupied. But then I thought twice about it and leaned against his desk.

"It was a really long time ago."

The phone rang and Cabel reached to answer it. Seeing that he was busy, I took my leave and walked away.

"I'll see you tonight," I whispered, heading out the door.

Cabel waved, and as I walked down the hallway alone, I caught a whiff from the trail her scent had left behind. A sweet perfume that smelled of cotton candy.

I felt sick to my stomach.

* * *

The fireplace burned with brightness and warmth, relaxing my worried mind. Jeremy let me off work early, perhaps sensing that I needed alone time with my husband. Cabel enjoyed having me home in time for dinner, a meal that we had found ourselves spending apart. It was an unfortunate habit that we had fallen into.

"Hey," Cabel chimed, walking into the room with a box of ornaments. The Christmas tree was up, though no thanks to me. I hoped that decorating it tonight would be a way to catch up on all that I was missing.

"Hey," I sweetly replied.

Cabel sat down on the sofa beside me and draped his arm over my shoulder. "Are you cold?" His eyes dropped to the blanket spread out across my lap.

"Not now."

The side of his mouth twitched as he tried to fight a crooked smile. With a complacent grin, I locked my arms around his torso and put my head on his chest. When he touched the side of my neck with his fingers, I closed my eyes and let myself drown in the comfort of his warmth.

"I miss you," I whispered, the tone of my voice blending with the hiss of the fireplace.

Cabel curled his arm around my back, then turned my chin up in the palm of his hand. When I wouldn't meet his eyes, Cabel dragged his thumb across my cheekbone, a firm, yet gentle touch. Trapped beneath his gaze, I looked up to find two spheres of cool ice staring back at me.

"You shouldn't," he countered.

Hurt by his words, I narrowed my eyes and went to pull away. But he kept my chin well within his grasp, and I was forced to listen to what else he had to say.

"But I miss you, too," he confessed, letting his fingertips descend my jawline and linger near my throat.

My face fell, but he cupped my cheek in his

hand, his eyes on mine, no matter how they wavered.

"It doesn't have to be like this." Cabel cooed, nestling his fingers in my hair.

Our eyes met, and I felt red hot blood coursing through my veins. Cabel looked at my mouth and swallowed, his intent and purpose as clear as mine.

"Kiss me," I begged, my line of sight falling to those lush, pillowy lips.

Cabel angled my face towards his and said, "I will as soon as you shut up."

His mouth pressed against mine, a slow, steady kiss that left me feeling quite the opposite. My hands braced his shoulders, as his fingers became twisted and tangled forces in my hair. Heat raised across every surface of my skin, leaving me flushed, especially when he sought to consume every breath I had left.

"Hmm." I felt the smile against Cabel's lips.

"I love it when you tell me what to do," Cabel whispered, his warm breath against my mouth.

"Really?" I mumbled between kisses.

"Yes," he hissed, hovering above me as my back sank into the couch. He clasped my hand in his and lowered his body to mine. "Really."

Chapter 3

Early in the morning, I woke up feeling refreshed, satisfied. Cabel lay beside me, his beautiful face like a work of art on the pillow. Every line, every plane was etched with the charm of natural good looks, of natural good fortune.

When the alarm went off, I leaned over his weary body and silenced that awfully horrendous succession of beeps. Cabel squirmed beneath me and grabbed the tops of my arms to hold me to his frame. I placed my hands on his torso and rested my chin on top of them, offering a fine view of my husband in the morning.

"I wish we didn't have to work."

"What?" I stared into his husky blue eyes, not believing a word he said.

"Today, I mean." He reached out to tap my nose with his finger, and I shut my eyes. "We never had a honeymoon."

I squinted my eyes and peered up at him, surprised by the sudden subject change. For some reason, I hadn't expected this to bother him. Surely, we weren't the first love birds to elope and then skip all of the postnuptial activities. Well, most of them anyway.

"I know." I held his gaze, and he scratched his head in confusion.

"You didn't want one?" He narrowed his eyes then added, "With me?"

"Of course I did."

"Then why didn't you just say that?"

Sighing aloud, I sat up in the bed and pushed the covers away.

"No." His fingers clamped down around my arm. "Don't ignore me."

Gnawing at the inside of my cheek, I saved my anger for another time and slid beneath the sheets. "It's not safe," I said, reclining on my elbows as I turned to the side and faced him.

"Finley, that was months ago. I'm sure whoever sent them has moved on to something else."

I shook my head and scowled.

"What? You don't believe me?"

"How can I when you don't even know what you're talking about?"

Cabel got out of bed and slipped into his sweatpants, then began the irritating process of pacing back and forth. "And you do?" he countered.

"Neither of us do, Cabel." I folded my knees into my chest and leaned against the headboard, the covers draped over my body. "That's why it's best to stay put."

Cabel nodded, but then he rolled his neck and moistened his lips. I knew there would never be an end to this.

"I want to take you somewhere." Cabel set his hands on his hips and looked me head on, his chest rising and falling with each intake of breath.

"Why?" I had never seen the importance.

We were married. We were happy. We were in love.

What else mattered?

"Because the only place we've ever been is this house!" He scowled and turned his head to the side, angry with himself for raising his voice at me.

"Not technically," I noted, catching his eyes as he chuckled, though not out of humor.

"You call that a honeymoon?"

I giggled and replied, "We were alone together in the middle of nowhere."

Cabel rocked back on his heels and ruffled a hand through his messy blonde locks. I got the feeling that there was more to this desperate need for a honeymoon. There was something that he wasn't telling me. But because I loved him, I let it go for now.

"Baby," I coaxed, sticking my lower lip out. "Come here." I patted the empty space in front of me on the mattress and grinned like a little girl when he gave in.

Cabel succumbed with a sigh and collapsed on the bed, as if he were an amateur diver content to buckle his knees and belly flop. Pleased, I let a Cheshire cat smile peel across my face and stroked my fingers through his hair. Cabel inched closer, hugging my waist and resting his head on my stomach. When he spoke, I felt the vibration of his voice through my skin.

"I just want to make you happy," he muttered under his breath.

"You do make me happy." I rubbed his head and then tilted it back so he was forced to look at me. "Cabel," I professed, "you do make me happy."

He shut his mouth and smiled, but the upwardly curving expression did not reach his eyes. When I secured his chin firmly within the palm of my hand, his crystal blue gems widened with delight.

"But if it's that important to you," I began, hardly able to finish my sentence. Cabel folded his arms at the back of my neck and pulled me towards him until his lips touched my cheek.

"I'll take you wherever you want," he insisted. "The Bahamas, Paris, Hawaii, Alaska," he prattled on.

"Why don't you decide?" I offered. "I'm sure wherever you pick will be great."

Cabel held my face in his hands, and I loved the way his skin warmed my cheek. Whether we had a honeymoon or not was of no importance to me. But if Cabel really wanted to take me on vacation to some faraway place, then I would go.

"You're my wife now," he explained, brushing stray hairs out of my eyes with his fingertips. "I don't want to deny you anything."

"You haven't," I assured him, rubbing the hard muscle in his arm.

Cabel leaned in to kiss me and uttered, "I won't."

It was a promise.

Chapter 4

Days passed, and my stress level increased. I had assignments due, research that wasn't done, and finals to take. Christmas was starting to look like the light at the end of the tunnel, and I couldn't wait to see it.

Since neither of us had any living relatives, I had no earthly idea how Cabel and I were going to spend the holidays. We were a pair of orphans who defined family by the mere presence of each other. Maybe we could drink hot cocoa and watch *It's A Wonderful Life* to get into the Christmas spirit. Wasn't that what everyone else did?

Before leaving campus for the day, I had the idea to run by the store and pick up a pair of stockings for us to hang over the fireplace. What did it matter if they were generic with no name stitched across the top? This was our first Christmas together, and I wanted to do it right.

After getting off the elevator, I made my way down the hall to Cabel's office. Sometimes, I still got butterflies in my stomach, remembering what it was like to head to his office as a student. But our lives were so much different now. Everything had changed.

I reached the cracked door and pushed it open, only to find Dr. Jane Adams hunched over Cabel's desk, standing suggestively close to my husband. He was seated in his office chair, his chin in his palm as he looked over the paperwork before him. Jane, however, stood beside Cabel with every part of her elevated figure angled towards his body.

"Hello," I spoke, my voice feeling very far away.

Jane's head snapped up at the sound, her golden blonde hair whipping in response. Cabel looked up to find me in the doorway and smiled, abandoning his chair to come greet me. As he walked over, I maintained my frozen posture, eyeing Jane and her red stilettos, red dress, red lips, red face. Didn't she own clothing in any other color?

"Hey, baby." Cabel held me at arm's length and planted a kiss on my forehead, but I wasn't so easily diverted. "Are you on your way out?"

"Yeah." I blinked, trying to regain my cognizance.

Jane remained in front of Cabel's desk, her arms crossed over her chest in annoyance. For the life of me, I couldn't fathom what she could be doing here. She wasn't expected to start teaching until January, so why was she in my husband's office? Again?

"I was just going to stop by the store on my way

home," I confessed, though my eyes never left Jane's. The way she cocked her head to the side and scanned my figure sent a chill pulsing down my spine. Unable to look away from her searing gaze, I was bombarded with questions in my mind.

Who was she? What was she doing here? And what did she want with my husband?

"Did you need anything?" I pulled my eyes away from Jane and peered up at Cabel. He looked serene, clutching my elbow in the palm of his hand, as if no one else was in the room but us. Couldn't he see what I saw? Couldn't he feel the tension in the room? Tension that had been caused by one person.

"No, I'm good. Thanks for asking though." He left a light kiss on my mouth and returned to his desk, leaving me lingering in the doorway like a fool. "I'll see you tonight."

"Okay," I croaked.

When Cabel sat down in his chair and pushed his sleeves back, Jane scribbled something onto a document with her pen and then handed it to him. I watched Cabel adjust his tie, look the document over, then move on to the next piece of information.

In my heart, I knew something was wrong. It was a gut feeling, a natural response, a simple case of women's intuition. And I couldn't ignore it.

On my drive to the store, I let my mind race with worries, stressors, negative thoughts. I couldn't stand the fact that another woman was working so closely with him, a woman his age, a woman from his past, a woman who had known Cabel before me.

Did she have the upper hand? After all, she was older, ivy league educated, advanced in her career. They were on the same level. She could relate to Cabel in ways that I just couldn't, especially since they would both be teaching in the same department next semester. Suddenly, I remembered Jane insinuating that her office would be located directly across the hall from his. Easy access. Constant appearances. Perpetual presence. That's what she would be in my husband's life. Could I handle that?

Shoving the matter off for the time being, I strolled through a department store and found a pair of stockings that were just right. The first was royal blue, covered in velvet, adorned with poinsettia applique patterns, while the second looked like it had been fashioned with the deep red and white trim off Santa's hat. I bought them both.

* * *

Sipping at a mug of hot cocoa, I sat alone on the couch in the living room and watched the fire. The way the embers grew reminded me of the raging hot jealousy that was rising up inside of me. Jane had an interest in my husband, though all that mattered was whether he could see it or not.

While I trusted Cabel, there was something

about Jane that made me question their time at Cornell together. How well had they actually known each other? According to the way Cabel acted towards her, Jane must have been nothing more than an old classroom acquaintance. Although it did come across as awfully familiar, the way they were around each other. I wondered, in their graduate school days, had either ever desired more from the other? And had the other ever given it?

Feeling restless, I set my cocoa down on a coaster over the end table, then rose from the coach and busied myself with the simple task of hanging our stockings. The one I had chosen for Cabel suited his features, the velvety smooth fabric a deep royal blue. The front was embellished with a scattering of appliques, some in the image of holly leaves, while the center design resembled the exact likeness of a poinsettia. My own stocking was a deep burgundy color, yet bore the same appliques as the first. Once I had hung them side by side over the fireplace, I admired my work with a silent smile. Despite everything that had happened in the past, Cabel truly was my family.

"Hello, Mrs. Jones."

My heart skipped a beat at the sound of Cabel's voice. He had snuck up behind me, making me wonder how long he had been standing there, watching. When his arms slipped around my stomach and he kissed the side of my face, I felt my cheeks blush with warmth.

"Did you get these today?" Cabel set his head on my shoulder and gestured to the pair of stockings over the fireplace.

"Yes," I said. "Do you like them?"

"Yes," Cabel firmly replied. "I do."

Grinning at his approval, I turned around in Cabel's arms and hung my head. Following my line of sight, Cabel's eyes searched my face, until he captured my elbow in his hand and caught on. "What's wrong?"

Averting his gaze, I let myself out of his grasp and strode towards the Christmas tree in the corner. Amid the blinking lights, I found a collection of ornaments hanging from the various branches as though a shopkeeper had intended for the tree to be showcased in the front window on display. Our Christmas tree had no character, no uniqueness, no defining fingerprint that made it our own. None of the decorations were custom, because they were the standard, generic, non-descript kind. In that moment, I realized that the tree was fit for staging houses, not filling homes.

"How well did you know Dr. Adams," I began, "at Cornell?"

I felt the tension expand between us before I even turned around. By the time I did, Cabel's face had altered to an expression of avoidance. Determined to fix my curiosity, I crossed my arms over my chest and met him eye to eye.

"What do you want to know that for?" he returned, dodging the question.

"She likes you," I noted. "I'm wondering if maybe there was a time when you liked her, too."

Cabel clenched his jaw and sighed. When he looked away, uneasiness settled in the pit of my stomach. If I was wrong about my assumptions, then why was there anything to hide?

"Well," I finally said once I grew tired of waiting. "Am I right?"

Cabel gnawed on the edge of his lip, then began pacing the floor in front of me. Every step made me feel all the more nauseous. If the truth was so bad that he couldn't even look me in the eye and tell me, then maybe I didn't want to know.

"Finley," Cabel reasoned, placing his hands on my shoulders as he came towards me. "You really don't need to know." He faked a smile.

"Maybe it's important to me."

Cabel groaned and shoved his hands into his pockets, then turned on his heel to face the fireplace.

"Maybe I want to know," I went on.

Cabel turned back to me and confessed, "But it doesn't matter anymore."

"It matters to me." I searched Cabel's face, as his icy eyes left mine. Desperate, I reached out and grabbed his arm to return his gaze to me. "Just tell me. Please."

Cabel glanced down at the hand I had placed on his arm. Then he pressed his lips together and sighed. When his eyes dropped to the floor and stayed there, I held my breath and then swallowed, waiting for his response.

"We used to be," he paused, bringing his eyes to me at the last, "together."

My body froze, cracking and disintegrating on the inside. I felt very warm all of a sudden. And when he turned away from me, letting my hand fall to my side, the fever spread.

"Together," I lilted, my throat uncomfortably dry. "You mean—"

"Finley," he sternly declared, as if he were correcting me. "You know what I mean."

Feeling like a stranger in my own home, I pressed my hand into the back of my neck to relieve the tension building there and watched Cabel take a seat on the couch. He leaned forward and braided his fingers together, avoiding my scrutiny. I didn't intend to have such a look of judgment and disapproval on my face, but shouldn't I know these things? His ex-girlfriend was about to become the new professor across the hall. The fact that he hadn't told me felt like a big fat lie. Even if it was technically by omission.

"Why didn't you tell me?" I uncrossed my arms from my chest, though I didn't remember crossing them in the first place.

Cabel lifted his head. "Because I didn't want to upset you."

"So you'd rather lie to me instead?"

"It wasn't a lie!" he demanded, turning his head to the side and gritting his teeth.

"Well, it certainly wasn't the truth." I felt

unsteady on my feet, like I was about to tip over. But I held on to what balance I could. We were arguing, and I had to be strong.

"I'm sorry, okay?" Cabel eyed me across the room, and I wished I didn't feel so betrayed. After such a long, stressful week, all I really wanted was to lie down in his lap and let him hold me. But now I felt defensive, on guard. The walls were back up.

When I stared into his eyes and failed to even open my mouth, Cabel rubbed his temples, his long fingers massaging either side of his face. I had never felt so torn before, because I wanted to touch him, but I didn't. I wanted him to touch me, but I didn't.

My emotions were like oil and vinegar in a jar, contained, yet not mixing together very well. I found myself wanting to leave just as much as I wanted to stay.

"Did you sleep with her?"

The question came out all wrong. That was not what I had meant to say, nor the kind of question I had intended to ask. But now that it was out there, I didn't want to take it back.

Cabel clenched his jaw and swallowed, his lips parting ever so slightly. When he pressed his palms together with such force that his knuckles turned white, I held my breath until he gave me an answer.

"Yes," he confessed. "We were engaged."

My eyes widened. My strength weakened. My

heart nearly stopped.

"What?" I slowly croaked, stumbling over the word to the extent that I could hardly get it out of my mouth.

His eyes reached mine and then flitted away. He couldn't stand to look at me, and I suddenly realized that my feelings towards him were much of the same. Wanting to be alone, I turned on my heel and fled.

"Finley, it didn't mean anything," he called after me as I left the room.

Racing up the staircase, I bolted into our bedroom and then retreated further into the adjoining bathroom, locking the door behind me. Once I saw myself in the mirror, the tears came streaming down my face. I ripped my clothes off and ran hot water in the tub, seeking out the scalding liquid as a way to numb my pain.

Didn't mean anything? *Didn't mean anything?* Cabel's words went round and round in my head, like a spinning top. How could it not mean anything? He had been engaged before. He had given someone else a ring. I thought I had been the only one to bear the name fiancé. How dare he act like it didn't matter! It would have been one thing if he had told me before, if he had just admitted the truth. But to find out this way? That Jane was not just some old classmate from his past or new co-worker in the office. She was his ex-fiancé, and the fact that Cabel had knowingly left me ignorant of the whole matter felt like a dagger to the heart.

"Finley!" Cabel banged on the bathroom door, while I sank into the steaming water and thanked the running faucet for masking the sound of my tears. "Open the door!"

"Leave me alone, Cabel!" I pulled my knees into my chest, wrapping my arms around my legs. "Just give me a chance to think!"

The banging stopped, as the voice on the other side of the door turned silent. When I knew he was gone, that he had left me in peace, the pain in my chest expanded. Somehow, the act of him walking away so easily left me wanting to cry buckets. If he cared, wouldn't he want to argue with me? Fight for me? Maybe he didn't care.

I sat in that bathtub for a very long time, until my fingers turned pruney and my body was shivering. When I unplugged the drain, the water seemed to escape so rapidly, like I had been holding it hostage, and it couldn't wait to break free and leave my naked body. Maybe that was how Cabel felt. Maybe that's why he didn't mind being in such close quarters with Jane. Maybe he wanted her there. Maybe he'd rather spend time with her than me. Or maybe, I had blown the entire thing out of proportion, because deep down, I knew Cabel was all I had.

After getting out of the tub to dry off, I wrapped the towel around me and opened the door gently. When I saw an empty bed in the dark bedroom, my bottom lip trembled and the tears returned. With a hand to my mouth, I sobbed aloud, tripping over something on my way to the closet. I felt a firm hand at the top of my back and looked up to find that I had fallen into my husband's lap.

"Cabel," I gasped, equally startled by his presence and worried that I had hurt him. "I'm sorry."

As I pulled away, Cabel grabbed me and tightened his grip on my arms. I caught my breath and gazed at his face, watching the way he admired me. Our eyes met, and the fact that he had been sitting outside the bathroom door this whole time was enough to do me in.

"No," he murmured, gently stroking my face. "I am."

Sighing aloud, I furrowed my brow and looked down, though he swiftly pulled my eyes back to his. Cabel cupped my cheek in the palm of his hand, and when he dragged his thumb along the edge of my lower lip, I shuddered. My hair hung in damp waves down my back, framing my face as I felt drops of water trickle down my chest.

"I should have told you and I didn't," Cabel admitted. "I'm sorry." He weaved his fingers through my hair and repeated, "I'm sorry."

Taking it all in, I rested my hands on his shoulders and breathed, "I'm sorry, too."

Cabel nodded, letting a hand descend the length of my arm. The touch of his cool skin to my warm flesh left me breathless, and when he looked into my eyes again, I knew that all I wanted in this world was him.

Chapter 5

During finals week, the library was a madhouse, so I sought out one of the labs in the psychology department where I could study in peace. Since it was after five in the afternoon, the room I chose was vacant, and I had my pick of the empty tables. Even though I had my own office in the grad lounge, I fared better when I wasn't surrounded by so many students.

About an hour into my study session, I heard the lock on the door click, as someone swiped their key card and pushed the door open. Mildly disappointed by the unexpected visitor, I kept my eyes on the open book in front of me and paid the newcomer no attention. That is, until the sound of her heels clicking against the floor caused pulsing in my ears.

Jane walked around the other side of the table and pulled a chair out. "Do you mind if I sit with you?"

Keeping my cool, I acknowledged her politely and motioned to the chair. "Go ahead."

With a pleasant grin on her face, she dropped a notebook and her purse onto the table and sat down.

I turned my eyes back to my work and kept my head down.

"So," she began, interrupting my studies, "getting ready for finals?"

"Yeah." I nodded.

"I remember my first semester of grad school. Really tough. I couldn't have gotten through it without Cabel."

I bit my tongue and dared to meet her eyes, though I didn't know how that would keep me from feeling provoked. "You went to Johns Hopkins, too?" I wondered, recalling that Cabel had received his master's there first. It was only later that he attended Cornell for his PhD.

"No." She jerked her head to the side as if I were an alien, then made a show of playing with her finely manicured nails. "Cabel was on the fast track, so he was getting his doctorate at Cornell by the time I started grad school."

"Oh," I clucked, "I see."

Jane smiled, and I wanted to slap the expression right off her face. I wondered if Cabel had told her that I knew. I knew that Cabel had once been hers, that now he was mine, that I had been the only one to elevate from fiancé to wife in the course of a day.

"How did you and Cabel meet?" Jane pressed, her blue eyes raging with fire.

Envy. Desire. Jealousy. She wanted what I had.

"I thought you weren't going to start teaching

until January," I noted. "So why are you here?"

She eyed me carefully, drumming her fingernails against the table. "Cabel and I are working on a project. We're thinking of co-teaching a class together next semester."

"Oh?" I held her gaze.

"Didn't he tell you?"

Flicking my eyes to the textbook before me, I let my mind run rampant with worrisome thoughts. Why didn't Cabel tell me? Perhaps he knew how I would feel. Perhaps he didn't want me to know. Perhaps she was lying.

"What do you want, Jane? Can't you see that I'm busy?" I held my chin high, determined to keep her from stomping all over me.

She narrowed her eyes at me and continued, talking as if she had never stopped.

"Isn't it odd that Cabel would marry someone right after graduation?" Jane examined her cuticles as she spoke. "Someone, who only weeks before, was a student? Someone, that at one time, was *his* student?"

Gritting my teeth, I glared into her eyes and held my tongue.

Jane hunched her shoulders and leaned forward. "I'm not concerned that you were accepted into the graduate program here because your husband is a professor. I know that's why you got in. What I'm wondering is how you didn't get Cabel fired when you were a freshman."

"Excuse me?"

"Isn't that how this all started? How the two of you met?"

I began packing my things and avoided the pressure she was putting me under. Since she had weaseled her way back into Cabel's life, what had he told her? Everything?

"You don't know what you're talking about."

"Really?" Jane stood and collected her things. "But don't I?" She paused before heading to the door and adding, "Mrs. Jones."

My heart was pounding as I stared at the floor, ready for her to leave so I could release the breath I had been holding. When her heels stopped clicking just before the door, I froze in place, glad that my back was to her.

"My name is Dr. Adams," she warned. "You may not be in undergrad anymore, but you're certainly not a professor."

I rolled my eyes at the ceiling and felt my pulse rising.

"And I know about what you did with Cabel, because I've been in your shoes."

I turned around in my seat to face her, much to her enjoyment.

"What do you mean?" I wondered, half-stressed, half-terrified.

"I know how he is, Finley," she said, passive and quiet. "I was his student, too."

Chapter 6

At the restaurant that night, I looked like a clumsy fool, sloshing drinks, fumble fisting around on a pair of left feet. Jeremy pulled me aside and cleared the kitchen, wanting to speak to me alone. When the last worker had passed through the swinging door, I leaned into the counter and sighed.

"What's going on, Finley?" he pressed, though it was hard for Jeremy's voice to come across as anything but gentle.

"Nothing," I replied, my eyes down.

"Finley," he nudged. "You're waiting on the wrong tables, knocking food trays over, and scaring the customers."

Hot air flared through my nostrils, while I crossed my arms over my chest and dug my nails into my flesh. I had been distracted all evening, thinking of Jane and what she had said. So she had been a student as well? What did that mean? Was this some game that Cabel liked to play, only I had been the first to make it to the finish line? I felt like the next item checked off someone's list, the next notch in his belt. If pursuing female students was something he had always done, then how many others were there?

"Finley," Jeremy called, waving a hand in front of my face.

I blinked and acknowledged his presence before me. "Sorry."

"What's with you today?"

"I don't know," I muttered. "I guess I'm just distracted is all."

"You could say that."

I looked into Jeremy's green eyes and glared. But there was nothing but light in those spheres of lime. He reached out to me and placed a hand on my shoulder. And that was when all of the churning emotions from the past few days came rising to the surface, and I broke down.

"Finley," Jeremy coaxed, pulling me into his arms and setting my head on his chest. "Shh, it's okay."

Letting go, I cried into Jeremy's shirt and relaxed in his embrace. Despite the fact that we were no more than friends, Jeremy had always been good to me. He had always been someone that I could trust and confide in. If he weren't the owner's son, I surely would have been fired a long time ago, especially during my first week, when it appeared that all I could do was fail. Unfortunately, it seemed that my rookie behavior had returned as of late.

"I think you need to take some time off," Jeremy suggested, patting my back reassuringly.

"What?" I lifted my head and searched his face, my eyes darting here and there. "You're firing me?"

"No," Jeremy insisted. "Of course not."

"Then why?"

Jeremy took a breath and sighed, gazing into my glistening eyes. He wiped a teardrop away before it could run down my cheek. I averted my gaze to the floor, but he turned my chin up in the palm of his hand.

"You're in the middle of finals week. You're stressed out. I get it." Jeremy pressed his thumb against my cheek. "And maybe there are some things that you don't want to tell me."

I caught the glint of understanding in his eyes and nodded.

"Well," he exhaled, tilting his head to the side as he took a step back. "Why don't you take the rest of the month off? Focus on grad school, and there will still be a job here waiting for you in January."

I looked him over with disbelief, not understanding his generosity.

"I'm not taking no for an answer." He grinned, remaining in my line of sight, even when I tried to turn away.

"Thank you, Jeremy." I stumbled into his embrace and gave him a hug. But then I thought of going home to Cabel tonight and realized what I was going to have to confront him with.

"If there's something going on," he whispered

in my ear, "you can tell me. You can always tell me."

I pulled away shaking my head, but Jeremy kept my arms in his grasp. "No, I'm fine."

He tugged at my chin and stared into my eyes. "Are you sure?"

"Yeah," I stuttered, wiping away what tears I had left. "I'm sure."

"All right." He stepped back and let me go, though I knew he didn't believe a word I had told him. But Jeremy had always been great like that. When I needed my time or space, he gave it to me.

"I'm sorry about tonight," I sobbed, forcing myself to cheer up and fake a smile.

"It's okay," he consoled, turning on his heel. "Just go home and get some rest. You look like you haven't slept in a while."

The swinging door swayed back and forth once he passed through it. Alone in the kitchen, I rocked back on my heels and gazed into the reflective surface of a metal bowl. Jeremy was right. I did look tired.

Maybe that was why Cabel had asked me to quit. Maybe it was nothing more than insanity to be burning the candle at both ends. Then again, maybe the exhaustion hadn't really started until the arrival of his old friend.

* * *

When I got home from work, I didn't expect

to find Cabel still up. But he was. So I trekked into his office where he was in the process of grading papers.

"Hi," he managed, not even bothering to look up. Under normal circumstances, I would have written his lack of excitement off as work-related. Tonight, on the other hand...

I sat down on the leather couch facing his desk and held my car keys in my hands. Trying to contain my emotions, I focused on the way the sharp ridges in the house key cut into my palm. It was a copy made from Cabel's key, and he had given it to me not long after we were married. Reflecting on that moment threatened to bring tears to my eyes, but I bit my tongue to keep them at bay.

"Finley," Cabel addressed, momentarily pausing his work. "What's wrong?"

With my eyes down, I squared my shoulders and said, "How many people did you tell about us?"

"What?" Cabel set his pen down, and when he leaned back in his office chair, I heard it squeak. "What do you mean?"

I levelled my eyes at him and glowered, but he did no more than shrug his shoulders.

"Jane," I explained. "She knows about us."

Cabel's arctic blue eyes widened, and even from where I was sitting, I could tell that his pupils had dilated.

"She knows how we met, I mean." I squirmed

in my seat and swallowed, not at all ready for this part of the conversation. "She told me that she was your student, too." I slowly lifted my eyes to meet his, because I was scared of what I might find in them.

"No, she wasn't," Cabel denied. "We were both in grad school at the same time."

I shook my head and wanted to cry. "Do you honestly expect me to believe you?"

Cabel scoffed, immediately taking offense. "Yes, I do." He waited a beat before adding, "Why wouldn't you?"

I looked up to find his eyes on mine. Somehow, he didn't look the same, and I was no longer sure if I knew my husband or not. And though I refused to accept it, that's what Jane had intended to leave me with today. Doubt.

"I don't know, maybe because you lied to me about the fact that your ex-fiancé is going to be working across the hall."

"I never lied," he countered.

"Yes, you did."

I rose from the couch and approached his desk, still fiddling with the keys in my hands.

Cabel inhaled, rubbing his face with his hand. In all honesty, he was just as tired as I was. But I didn't care. I wanted the truth. And I wanted my husband back.

"What do you expect?" I posed, standing closer. "Who am I supposed to believe?"

"Your husband," Cabel argued, rising to his

feet.

With a smug nod, I turned on my heel to leave, but Cabel walked around his desk and came after me. Before he could say anything, I beat him to it.

"Look, I'm tired, and I'm going to bed."

Cabel took a step closer and backed me into the foyer. "You don't get to decide when we're done with this conversation."

"Well I am done with it, and I'm going to bed," I barked back. "Good night."

As I headed for the staircase, Cabel grabbed my arm and jerked me back to him. "Did you ever think that I might be the one who's actually telling the truth? That Jane is the one who's lying, not me?"

Furious, I yanked my arm out of his hold and slammed my palms into his chest. "Get away from me!"

Cabel staggered back, glancing over me with shock. I caught my breath and tried to cast my anger aside. But it was just so hard.

"If she's lying, then how does she know about us? Did you tell her?" I considered.

"No, of course not."

"Well then how does she know?"

"Finley," he snickered, hovering over me. "You were my student. We got married right after you graduated. What are people supposed to think? It's not too hard to figure out."

"What are you saying? That everyone thinks

the only reason I got accepted into the graduate program is because I married my professor?"

"No, and we did nothing wrong." Cabel placed his hand on my shoulder. "But people talk. What I'm wondering is why you care what they think."

Angry with his honesty, I huffed my way up the staircase, ignoring the fact that he wasn't behind me. He could stay downstairs in his office and grade papers all night for all I cared. I would be just fine sleeping alone.

Sauntering into the bedroom, I changed out of my work clothes and went straight to bed. When I heard the door open a couple hours later, I pretended to be asleep, though I had yet to shut my eyes. Cabel quietly crept into the room and stripped his shirt off. Sensing that someone was watching him, Cabel turned around to find that I was still awake. Without a trace of frustration left in his body, Cabel sat down on the edge of the bed and touched my face with his hand.

"Why didn't you tell me about her?" I whispered, the malice I had felt before no longer present in my voice.

"Because there was nothing I could do about it," he said. "I can't keep the university from hiring her."

I relaxed beneath the covers and stared up at the ceiling, knowing that I believed everything Cabel had told me. It was simple. Cabel was my husband, and I loved him.

"Did you love her?" I don't know what

compelled me to ask such a question. But once again, I found myself glancing back at him, waiting to hear the answer.

"At the time, I thought I did." He raised his eyebrows and then leaned down over me. "But I don't anymore." When I lowered my eyes, Cabel cupped my cheek in his hand. "Nothing has ever been as good as it is with you. I may have loved her back then, but I love you more." He stretched out beside me and planted his lips on my neck. "I love you more than I've ever loved anyone else."

"Wait," I stalled, separating his mouth from my throat. "Why didn't you marry her? Who called it off?"

Cabel sat back on the mattress to remove his shoes and socks. "I did."

"Why?"

Cabel stilled beside me, and I watched the way the moonlight scattered across his bare back. His muscles were firm and taut, beautifully sculpted. And I wanted to kiss every last one.

Cabel turned around and took my hand in his. "She wasn't who I thought she was."

"And am I?" I questioned.

"Yes." Cabel touched the side of my neck, and before I knew it, his fingers were caressing my jawline. "You are."

Chapter 7

When the day of my last final arrived, I skipped out of that exam room like a kid off to Candy Land. I had survived my first semester of grad school, and I couldn't be more excited. All I wanted to do was run upstairs and tell Cabel. It was after seven o'clock, and I knew he must be hungry. As soon as he was done with his duties as a professor, our vacation as a couple could truly begin.

On my way down the hall, I continued skipping like a fool, until the door to Cabel's office opened, and Jane came into view. I froze immediately, altering my steps to a slower pace. She giggled and waved into the open doorway, then started walking my way. I forced the taste of bile down my throat at the scent of her cotton candy perfume.

"Hello, Finley," she chirped, clutching the handbag over her shoulder. "What are you doing here so late?"

I avoided the condescending tone and merely smiled. "Just here to see my husband."

"Well." She peered down at me, sizing me up

from head to toe, making it clear that she did not view me as an equal. "How nice."

I breathed a sigh of relief when she scuttled away, channeling Miranda from *The Devil Wears Prada.* I hurried the rest of the way to Cabel's door and said a quick prayer for the future female students of Dr. Jane Adams.

"Hey," I sweetly chimed, letting myself in.

Cabel stretched his neck and glanced up from his work, brightening as soon as he saw me. Any other day, I would be livid that Jane had just left, and I could still smell her perfume lingering in the room. But Cabel and I had talked, and he wanted no one but me. I had no doubt in my mind that he would remain faithful.

"Why don't I pack all of this up and bring it home? We can get Chinese for dinner," he suggested.

"Sounds good." I rubbed my stomach, as it was already growling with hunger. Since this afternoon, I had consumed no more than some water and a Clif bar. "I'm starving."

"I bet you are." Cabel smirked, motioning towards me with his hand. "Come here."

Filling with warmth, I sashayed over to my beautiful man and reached for his body. He grabbed my arm and pulled me into his lap before I could wrap it around him.

When our lips met, I pushed my palm into his chest, but Cabel grabbed my wrist and squeezed. Blushing, I tried to rear back until he clasped his hands together at the small of my back. As his mouth worked over mine, twisting and kissing and crushing, I squirmed in his lap, unable to fully relax since we were at my school and his work.

"Cabel," I groaned when he gave me a chance to breathe. "No. Not here."

"Baby," he whined, dragging his fingernails down the length of my arm, teasing and coaxing.

Before I knew it, his fingers were wrapping around the back of my neck, and I let my mouth return to his like a pair of magnets. Cabel toyed with the hem of my shirt, slipping his hand beneath the barrier the cloth had created over my skin. When I leaned back to push his hand away, Cabel brushed his lips over my neck, soon reaching the throbbing pulse point just beneath my jawline. As my eyes shut in a silent surrender, his hands slithered up and down my bare back.

"Okay," I succumbed, breathing heavily.

Cabel picked me up and laid me down on the desk, stray papers flying to the floor. When my head touched the hard surface beneath me, I spread my arms to clear the remaining office supplies away. But then I caught sight of something strange, something that had been hidden beneath a stack of papers, something that made me feel sick.

"What's this?" I wondered, my eyebrow quirking in Cabel's direction. He froze in place, as I sat up on his desk and narrowed my eyes in his direction. "What is this?" I snapped, gritting my teeth in aggravation.

"It's nothing," Cabel insisted, running his fingers through his unkempt hair.

"Nothing?" I looked down at the object in my hand and glared.

Underneath that stack of papers on Cabel's desk, I had found an apple. Ripe. Green. Perfectly polished. Stunningly smooth. It was most likely a Granny Smith. Not quite sour, yet undoubtedly tart. The kind of fruit that would make you clench your jaw when biting into it. The kind that left your memory marked.

"You told her," I accused, my voice surprisingly soft for the way I was feeling.

"What?" Cabel blinked twice, disappointing me.

"I thought that was our thing," I croaked, my lower lip trembling.

Cabel shook his head, those blue eyes like floating glaciers that had started to sink. "I don't know what you're talking about. Jane just—"

"Save it," I clipped, sliding down from his desk. Ready to cry, I adjusted my clothes and grabbed my bag.

"Finley, wait! Where are you going?"

"Home," I said, my back to him.

"Okay, and how am I supposed to understand what just happened?"

Sighing aloud, I shut my eyes briefly and then opened them again before turning around to face him. When I did, his brow was furrowed, and his hands were on his hips. Swallowing, I looked down at the apple in my hand and set it on his desk. Then I turned it around to face him, so he could see for himself what he already knew had been imprinted on the peel.

Cabel glanced down at the apple and flitted his eyes up to me with surprise. But I was not going to buy into his feigned portrayal of suspense. He couldn't fool me. Not anymore.

"Finley," he demanded. "I've never seen that before in my entire life."

"Oh, really?" I countered. "You make a habit of not checking things on your desk?"

"Look, I've been busy administering exams. She said that it was left over from her lunch and put it on my desk. I had my head buried in a pile of work when she came in here."

"How convenient," I scoffed at his excuse.

"What do you want me to say?"

"The truth."

"That *is* the truth!"

I took a deep breath and turned away. "So you're telling me that you knew nothing about this—this," I stuttered, struggling to find the words.

"No," he interrupted. "I didn't even get a good look at it until just now."

I felt his eyes searing into my back, but I couldn't look back at him. I didn't know what to believe. I didn't know who to believe. But I really wanted to believe him.

"Listen, Finley, I'll talk to her. I'll tell her to

back off. I don't know what she wants."

Shaking my head, I turned on my heel to face him and said, "I do."

When he saw my eyes on him, the way I was admiring the view from afar, he shoved his hands into his pockets and took a step towards me.

"Don't." I held my hand up in the air. "I need to think." I opened the door and said, "Give me some space."

As I left his office and retreated to the parking garage, my insides felt like mush. All I wanted to do was cry, and by the time I got on the road, I couldn't have withheld my tears if I had tried.

Despite everything, I knew that Cabel had been faithful to me. Surely, I would have been able to smell her on his clothes, sense the dishonesty in his smile, see the unfaithfulness in his eyes. But none of that was the case. Cabel was mine. I just didn't know for how long.

Jane was trying to get her hooks in my husband. The fact that he no longer wanted her had burned a hole right through any sense of propriety she might have once had. She may have been Cabel's fiancé, but I was his wife.

* * *

When I arrived home, I headed upstairs and went straight to bed. I had skipped dinner, but after everything that had happened, I was no longer hungry.

If it had only been the apple that I had found

on his desk, buried beneath a stack of papers, I wouldn't have said anything. I wouldn't have accused him, because I wouldn't have made the connection to Jane. But on the face of the apple, like a harsh slap in the face, had been a red lipstick stain in the shape of a kiss.

Her lips had touched that apple, just as they wanted to touch him. I cringed at the very thought, burying my head beneath the covers. The semester was over, but she would be back in January. Teaching. Flirting. Strutting in and out of my husband's office since hers was only across the hall, a few footsteps away. Why had she applied for a teaching position at the exact same university where Cabel worked? Why did she have to come here and ruin everything?

I heard the front door click shut and knew that Cabel was home. When he climbed up the staircase, I pressed my face deeper into the pillow, dreading the argument to come. I felt deadlocked. I didn't want to make a decision. It wasn't that I didn't trust Cabel or had even accused him of anything. I just didn't know what to feel. What if Jane succeeded in taking him away from me? What if he let her?

"I got Chinese," Cabel announced, rattling the bag so I could hear.

My head remained hidden beneath the covers, and I closed my eyes. But then the bed dipped down as Cabel took a seat on the edge of the mattress. I held my breath until he peeled the blankets back to reveal my startled face.

"What are you doing?" He leaned over the bedside table and flicked on the lamp.

I pressed my palms into the mattress and sat up, leaning against the headboard. Cabel loosened his tie, and I noticed the way he was clenching his jaw. There was a fresh layer of stubble on his face, which any other night, I would have stroked my fingers over willingly.

"Well?" he cornered me, holding me in place with that piercing gleam in his eyes.

"I was tired, so I went to bed."

"Did you eat dinner?" He leaned back on his elbow, narrowing the distance between us.

"I'm not hungry."

Cabel sighed, raising his eyebrows. He looked at the window, though the blinds were drawn, and I lay still beneath the sheets. When the silence between us became too much, he spoke up in a sharp manner, drawing my focus back to him.

"What am I supposed to do, Finley?" he asked. "What do you want me to do?"

"First of all, I want you to stop acting like everything's fine, like this is normal. Stop pretending Jane doesn't want you back. She's your ex-fiancé and she works across the hall. How do you expect me to feel?"

I hadn't meant to respond with such bitterness. But it came out that way, and I couldn't take it back now. Realizing the rapid rise and fall of my chest, I made an effort to calm down, but I was too riled up now.

"So you're just going to blame everything on me?" He sat up and stared at the floor, his back to me, as he lingered on the edge of the bed.

"No, I'm not blaming everything on you, but—"

"Then why do you keep accusing me of something I haven't even done?"

"Cabel," I said, lowering the sound of my voice. "I'm not accusing you of anything."

"Really?" he probed, rising to his feet. "You could have fooled me."

Cabel turned the lamp off and grabbed the bag of Chinese food he had placed on the bed. When he walked out of the room, I found myself alone in the darkness. Scowling at my own hatred, I ripped the covers back and put on my satin robe before scurrying downstairs after him.

With a deep breath, I walked into the kitchen, and at the sound of my steps, Cabel froze. But after a few moments had passed, he resumed unpacking the bag of Chinese food and retrieved a fork and spoon from the silverware drawer. Thinking that we had returned to the silent treatment again, I took a step back and hesitated.

"I should have told you about Jane, all right?" Cabel confessed. "But you know now, and I've apologized." He turned back and looked over his shoulder at me. "I don't love her anymore," he insisted. "I haven't loved her in a very long time. All I want is you."

Gnawing on the edge of my lip, I took one step

forward with a furrowed brow. When Cabel saw that I wasn't going to take another, he leaned against the counter and stared.

"Is that not enough, Finley?"

I swallowed and looked into his eyes for the briefest moment. I didn't know what to do. I just felt so confused.

"I don't know," I muttered, tears stinging my eyes. Somehow, it seemed like Jane had accomplished what she had wanted to all along. To take what Cabel and I had and slowly tear it apart.

"Do you not trust me?" Cabel walked towards me, and I couldn't stand the aching warmth surrounding my heart. Ever since Jane had stepped into the picture, my thoughts were swimming with doubt. There was a difference between what I wanted to believe and all of the other possibilities.

"No, I do," I whispered, rubbing a hand over my face.

"Then what is it, baby? Please, talk to me," he begged.

"I don't know what to say." My lower lip trembled, and Cabel pulled me into his arms, tucking my head beneath his chin. My hands lay sandwiched between our torsos, as he ran his fingers through my hair. Before I could cry, he claimed my mouth, and his hand slid down my body.

At Cabel's touch, all I could think about was

the fact that he had once been doing the exact same thing to Jane. Consoling her. Touching her. Kissing her. Loving her. The mental image of their past life together left me seething and jealous. So I pulled away from him before he could completely hold me under his spell.

"No," I announced, lifting my hand to him like it was a stop sign.

Cabel let go of me and took a step back, his eyes on the ground as he placed his hands in his pockets.

"I'm sorry," I stuttered. "But I just can't." I wrapped my arms around my body, hugging myself to provide some comfort. "I can't stop thinking about you with her and—"

"How can you hold that against me?" he chastened, smoldering in a way that would make any girl look at his cheekbones and want to eat off them. "That was before I met you."

"I don't care," I sobbed, my voice laced with bitterness. Gazing into his eyes, I blinked at my blurry tears and asked, "Why did you have to sleep with her?"

When my throat felt dry and the lump that was settling there grew more painful, I turned on my heel and ran up the staircase. Even as I retreated into the bedroom to count my tears and hide, I knew that Cabel would come after me. He always did.

"So I'm being punished," Cabel continued, gliding over the threshold. "For something that I did years ago, before we even met."

"I don't expect you to understand," I growled in the dark, raising my voice. "It's easy for you to say things like that when you're the only one who's had me."

Cabel set his hands on his hips and exhaled.

"What if the roles were reversed?" I suggested. "What if Jeremy wasn't just someone I worked with at the restaurant? What if he was someone that I used to kiss and touch and love?" I stroked the stubble along Cabel's chin and jawline with my fingertips. "What if we used to—?"

"That's enough!" Cabel glowered down at me, firmly grasping my wrist in his hand.

I gritted my teeth and rubbed my bottom lip over the top. Casting my anger, jealousy, and mixed emotions aside, I looked into his eyes and inhaled. "I saved myself for you. Can't you appreciate that?"

Holding his jaw taut, Cabel breathed in and out, searching my face. I parted my lips, and his eyes dropped to my mouth. Eyes that had never been more full of desire.

As I steadied my breathing, Cabel's hand went around my neck, and he pulled me in by the back of my head. His other hand slithered around my waist to loosen my robe, while he mercilessly crushed his lips to mine. The sheer force of his desire sent me forward on the tips of my toes, but he took the shortening distance between us as a sign of my absolute consent.

His fingers slipped across my bare shoulders, and he pushed my robe down my back until it gracefully dropped to the floor. The sensation of his hands skimming down the length of my arms made me shudder. When Cabel noticed the way I was affected by his touch, he gently caressed the edge of my jawline with the pad of his thumb. A hushed breath of air passed through my lips as I shut my eyes.

Appearing off balance, I sank into Cabel's body, and he fisted his hand in my hair until our mouths met once again. My arms remained at my sides, since I had yet to reach out and touch him. The absence of my hands wrapping around his neck or twisting through his hair had quite an effect on Cabel. For the first time, he was completely on the offense, coming after me with everything he had.

"No," I murmured, turning my head away. No matter how desperately my body longed for Cabel, I couldn't get those muddled, unclear thoughts out of my head.

I opened my eyes and Cabel stood before me in shock, wholly angered and upset. Surely, he was taken aback that I had denied him twice in the past half hour. He wasn't used to being told no.

"You've never turned me down before," he rasped, pressing his forehead against mine.

"I'm confused," I said. "I need time to think."

Cabel lengthened the widening gap of space between us and looked down at me. From the expression on his face, I couldn't tell if he was more stunned or pained. Either way, I had wounded him. And even I knew that no one could hurt him as badly as I could.

"You don't want me anymore?" His breath rushed over my face, as I failed to ignore the wave of tingles drifting across my skin.

"Cabel, that's not it," I griped.

Stepping away from him, I tried to regain my posture and whatever sense of willpower I had left. But then Cabel moved closer, and I didn't know if I could keep resisting him. At some point, I would inevitably give in. I wouldn't be able to help it.

"Then what is it?" he snapped.

I intended to move around him, but Cabel blocked any chance of escape and grabbed my arms.

"I'm your husband," he warned, his voice dark, tempting, husky.

Levelling my eyes at him, I jerked my arms away and slammed them into his chest. "My husband?" My rage increased as I pushed him back again. "Well I guess that means that I'm your wife!"

Cabel clasped my elbow in his hand and tugged. "You *are* my wife! My wife and nobody else's."

Cabel crashed into me and fixed his mouth on mine, while I coiled my arms around him. His hands roamed up and down my back, searching and seeking, until he grabbed the backs of my thighs and lifted me off the floor. I captured his bottom lip between both of mine and whimpered when he tossed me on the bed.

Out of breath, Cabel climbed across the mattress and began unfastening the buttons on his shirt. I reached out for him and brushed my lips over his until he reared back. Confusion flitted across my face until I recognized the look in his eyes. Cabel wanted me to say the word.

"Yes," I sighed.

He leaned forward without hesitation and returned his mouth to mine.

Chapter 8

I'm sorry." I stroked the stubble along Cabel's jawline and kissed his neck.

He traced patterns over my back with his hand and said, "I thought I was going to have to sleep downstairs." We laughed, as he cupped my cheek in the palm of his hand.

"I've been overreacting a lot lately," I confessed. "And I'm sorry."

"I'm sorry, too." Cabel swiped his thumb along my cheekbone and smiled.

"I'm hungry," I declared, abrupt and terse.

He chuckled and shook his head at me.

"What?"

"You're a handful," he jabbed.

"And you're not?" I countered.

"Touché."

Still brimming over with joy, we got dressed and headed downstairs. The Chinese food had gotten cold, but I sat down on the countertop and grabbed a fork, not minding the absence of heat. Cabel stood in front of me and devoured a box of sweet & sour chicken. We shared the rice, and I fed Cabel some of my beef with broccoli when he was still hungry.

He rested his hand on my thigh as I wiped a drop of sauce from the corner of his mouth. Cabel kissed me then, and I had nearly forgotten about Jane. If only I could have erased her from my mind. Permanently.

"Maybe I should talk to the Department Head. About everything with Jane."

"What will he say?" I furrowed my brow.

"I don't know. But she left an apple on my desk with a lipstick stain. That's not exactly what you'd call appropriate work behavior. Plus, we were involved."

"Don't remind me," I scowled.

"And I'm married," he continued. "I'm not saying that I'm trying to make her lose her job. But if she tries anything, I'll have already alerted my boss."

"Do you think she will," I wavered, "try anything, I mean?"

"Not when her supervisor is watching her like a hawk."

Sensing that we were finally on the same page, I folded my arms around him and pulled him close. "Thank you, Cabel." I kissed the side of his neck, and he patted my back.

Cabel held me at arm's length and gazed into my eyes. "I don't trust her."

I rubbed his shoulders and said, "I don't either."

Swallowing, Cabel threw the empty bag of

Chinese food in the trash along with all of the containers. Then he washed his hands in the sink, while I sunk my teeth into my lower lip.

"It was never you, Cabel," I confessed. He turned the faucet off and looked back in time to hear me say, "I trust you."

He took my face in his hands, and I really didn't mind that they were still wet. "I know," he whispered.

Relieved that we had finally pushed our relationship forward, I brought his mouth to mine, and the honeymoon began.

Chapter 9

C abel went into the office the next day to finalize grades before we left for our vacation, the first romantic getaway we had ever had. In my mind, it was more of a second honeymoon, but in Cabel's, it was our first. When I started packing for the trip, thrills raced through me, because I hadn't been this excited in a very long time. Both of us had been working incredibly hard this semester. We deserved a break. We had earned it.

After breakfast, I organized the closet so it would be especially tidy when we returned from wherever we were going. I didn't like coming home to a messy house, and Cabel held the exact same view, neat freaks that we both were. But as I grabbed a bathing suit to pack in my suitcase, I suddenly felt uneasy.

Stumbling back on my feet, I pressed my palm into my forehead and felt of the dewy moisture there. When the uneasiness in my stomach spread to nausea, I ran into the bathroom and wretched into the toilet bowl. Sitting back against the wall, I closed my eyes and focused on my breathing. By the time the queasy feeling had escaped me, I flushed the toilet and washed my hands in the sink. After rinsing my mouth out and brushing my teeth, I resumed my packing in the closet.

An hour later, the feeling returned. And by the afternoon, I found myself nervously fidgeting in the waiting room of a doctor's office.

"Finley Jones?" a nurse called, standing in the open doorway that led back to the examination rooms.

Rising to my feet, I strolled into the hallway and clutched my purse over my shoulder. The last time I had been to the doctor was when I broke my foot, and Cabel had coerced me into seeing one. Strangely, that didn't seem like that long ago, though it had been years. In that amount of time, things between Cabel and I sure had made a drastic change.

Once the nurse directed me into a room, I sat down on the elevated examination table and heard the crinkly tissue paper adjusting beneath me. My mind felt unstable, lost in some other place, as I was prodded and poked, tested and questioned, scrutinized and examined. By the time a doctor was standing in front of me instead of a nurse, I hardly knew the difference.

"Mrs. Jones," she snipped, tearing me out of my daydream. The woman sounded impatient, and I wondered if this wasn't the first time she had called my name.

"Yes," I replied, turning my attention on her.

Her hair was a natural shade of dishwater blonde and cut like a schoolboy's. By the look in her tired gray eyes, I could fathom that I had become a nuisance in her tightly scheduled day. Feeling like a child, I let my shoulders sag forward and watched the next set of words leave her mouth.

"I said you're pregnant," she announced.

"What?" I was surprised by how low I was speaking, as well as the fact that I had barely moved a muscle. Truthfully, I was in shock.

"You're pregnant," she repeated. "Your last period was six weeks ago. The nurse marked it down on your chart."

Blindly staring ahead, I looked at the clipboard in her hand and failed to breathe. The nurse had asked questions about monthly planning and menstrual cycles, but I hadn't thought anything of it at the time. In fact, for the past half hour, I had been in a complete daze.

"Finley."

"Yes." I looked up, nodding all of a sudden. The world seemed to be spinning beneath my feet, and I couldn't catch myself.

"Congratulations." She smiled, and it was the first time I had seen her show any kind of emotion.

"Thank you. I—I don't know what to say."

"I'm guessing this wasn't a planned pregnancy?"

"No, not that. It's just..." My eyes sank to the floor, and I was drifting.

"If you haven't been taking proper precautions," she began, but I cut her off before she could insinuate anymore.

"No, we have. It's just sometimes..."

The doctor's smile widened, and I bit my tongue.

What was I supposed to tell her? Sometimes we got carried away? Sometimes we just couldn't wait? Sometimes neither of us thought to reach for what lay inside the nightstand drawer?

"Well, I just..." My cheeks were blushing scarlet red. I knew that much for sure. But what was there to be embarrassed about? After all, we were *married.*

"I just wasn't expecting that."

The doctor nodded, and she turned around to wash her hands in the sink. I wondered what she must think of me. They had asked me to pee in a cup. Since there was a need for a urine sample, shouldn't I have figured that one out?

"I'm just wondering why you didn't think of it yourself. That you might be pregnant, I mean."

Nervously fiddling with my hands, I forced a laugh and smiled. "I'm in grad school, and I just finished finals."

"Oh." She reached for a paper towel and dried her hands off. "I see."

Relieved that she didn't think I was crazy, I felt my body relax for the rest of the visit. I would need to make an appointment with an OBGYN, but she gave me some general advice from her own experience as a pregnant woman, and I gladly took the list of acceptable foods to eat when she offered it. My thoughts were spinning as she discussed the importance of prenatal vitamins. Despite the surprise, I truly was excited.

All that was left to do was tell Cabel.

Chapter 10

Too impatient to tell him at home, I drove straight from the doctor's office to campus. My heart was pounding as I stepped on the elevator in the psychology building. What was he going to think? While we had never discussed children before, I'd never had a doubt in my mind that Cabel wanted them. And even though the pregnancy might put grad school on hold, if only towards the end, I didn't feel disappointed in the slightest. I knew that there would be a way to figure it all out.

When the elevator chimed and I stepped off onto the fourth floor, I felt giddy, like a little girl again. In all the time of our relationship, nothing had ever felt like this. We had created a life together, and I was bursting with joy. In my wildest dreams, I had never imagined it would be like this.

Not thinking to knock, I opened the door to Cabel's office and walked right in. But the expression of sheer bliss that had been plastered on my face was immediately swept away with whatever sense of happiness I had felt. Jane was in Cabel's office, and when I entered, her lips were unmistakably planted on his.

Frozen in place, my heart sank from my chest to my stomach, and I had never felt more sick. When Cabel pulled away and caught me staring in the doorway, my hand clamped over my mouth and I ran.

"Finley!" Cabel called after me. "Finley!"

Letting the tears flow, I raced down the hallway and escaped into the elevator. Cabel was on my heels, but I didn't care. No matter how much he yelled my name, nothing could take away the pain. I felt betrayed, because I had been.

"Finley!"

I stabbed the button for the ground floor, and the doors closed before Cabel could pass through them. Holding on to the railing, I sank down to the floor and started to hyperventilate. When the tears came pouring down, I was overcome by a round of heaving sobs.

Despite my better judgment, I had noticed the signs, confronted Cabel, and like a fool, believed him. Ripping my hands through my hair, I thought about last night, how easily it had been for him to seduce me, to charm me, to pull me back under his spell. I had given in to him, even though my mind had been clouded with doubt. I had believed him because I respected him. I had believed him because I loved him.

When the elevator stopped and the doors slid open, I hurried off and headed for the exit. Cabel burst out of the stairwell and trailed me, but I rushed outside and into the parking garage. He kept calling my name, but I didn't want to hear it. I didn't want to hear anything he had to say.

"Finley, wait!" Cabel grabbed my arm before I reached my car and jerked me back. "Please, let me explain."

"Let go of me!" I hit him across the chest with my handbag until he released me. Then I climbed into my car and drove off, while Cabel banged on the window and chased after the car until I sped away.

Sniffling, I dried my eyes and paid attention to the speed limit on the way home. But my desire for safety on the highway came out of a need to protect the life of my unborn child, not my own. I pushed the news of the pregnancy back to the farthest corner of my mind, because if I tried to think about that right now, my head was going to explode.

As soon as I entered the house, my keys and handbag fell to the floor. I slipped out of my shoes and lay down on the couch in the living room with a blanket over my body and a pillow behind my head.

Out of the corner of my eye, I spotted the Christmas tree we had decorated together, as well as those stupid stockings that I had convinced myself would make us feel like a normal family during the holidays. What was I thinking? Nothing about the way Cabel and I had met or fallen in love or become husband and wife had been normal. And yet, looking back now, I wished that I had appreciated that time more. Turning my head, I cried into the pillow and nestled beneath the covers.

When the front door slammed, I flinched, hearing the sound of Cabel's footsteps in the foyer. He trudged into the living room and shook my arm until I peeked my head over the blanket. There were tears in my eyes, and when he lifted my chin with his finger, I slapped his hand away and glared.

"Just let me explain." Cabel knelt down in front of the couch, but I rolled over onto my side and stared at the wall.

"Don't touch me," I growled when he set his hand on my back.

What I had feared had been right all along. Jane still wanted Cabel. And whether he would admit it or not, there was a part of Cabel that still wanted Jane.

"I met with the Department Head today. He talked to Jane afterwards, so when she came into my office, I thought she wouldn't have the nerve to talk about anything but work. She started arguing with me about getting her in trouble. And when I asked her to leave, she kissed me. That's when you walked in."

I lowered my gaze and stayed still.

"That's all," he confessed. "That's everything that happened."

Taking it all in, I closed my eyes and tried not

to cry. No matter how badly I wanted to believe him, I just couldn't. Not this time.

"Finley." Cabel took a breath, and I could feel him moving closer. "Say something," he begged.

His hand caressed the back of my neck, as he pushed my hair over my shoulder.

"Finley," he crooned, his sweet breath ghosting over the side of my face.

"No!" I snapped, clenching my jaw and quivering before him.

"Baby, please. Believe me."

My heart felt like a marshmallow, gooey and soft, slowly melting beneath the fire in his eyes. But I couldn't let him do this to me. Not now. Not anymore. Not ever again.

With the blanket wrapped around me, I left Cabel in the living room and went upstairs, where I shut myself in the bedroom and hid beneath the covers. Regardless of my anger, I had left the door unlocked. But Cabel didn't come to bed that night. And when I woke up the next morning, he was gone.

Chapter 11

The phone rang, and I did *not* want to answer it. Not because it might be Cabel. Not because he had already called and left messages. But because all I wanted to do was lie in bed all day and sleep.

Ignoring the noise, I took a hot bath and ended up downstairs rifling through the pantry and fridge. I was starving and had the worst migraine that I had ever experienced in my entire life. Once I settled on canned soup and crackers, the phone rang again, and I couldn't stand the sound of it anymore.

"What?" I shouted into the receiver.

"Finley? Hey, it's Monty. Is this a bad time?"

I shut my eyes and shook the phone in my hand.

Dear Ol' Monty. While we hadn't exactly gotten off on the right foot, Cabel and I were indebted to the man. Once I graduated and became Cabel's wife, Monty had warmed up to me. But I never could forget what he had once said, that Cabel and I weren't right for each other, that it would never work out, that in the end, I would see.

Regardless, Monty was an old family friend of Cabel's. And since Cabel didn't have much family left, that meant a lot.

In recent years, Monty had maintained a career in politics. Currently, he was an active senator/presidential hopeful. He campaigned hard and well in advance, since the current head of state was in mid-term. Sure, Monty may have been a celebrity, but it never felt that way to me. He was the man who had saved our lives, especially the life of my husband. For that reason alone, I had welcomed him into our home when he was in town and answered his calls when he couldn't stop by. We had last spoken a few weeks ago, but that hardly seemed relevant now.

"No, it's not a bad time." I leaned into the kitchen counter and watched the soup simmering on the stove. "How are you?"

"Fine. Thank you for asking. Are you and Cabel holding up all right?"

"Sure," I sneered. "So what's going on?"

"Well, I'm in town, and I thought about dropping by."

"Cabel's not here, but I wouldn't mind keeping you company until he gets home." In all honesty, Monty was the best cure for my sour mood. He could distract me with memories of how Cabel and I used to be.

"Actually, it's probably best that he's not. There's something we need to discuss. Something about him."

"Okay..." I dragged out the word, an uncomfortable feeling in my gut.

"I'm heading there now. See you soon."

The phone line went dead as I searched the kitchen, my eyes drifting and wandering, just like my precarious thoughts. I tried not to worry too much about the conversation until Monty actually showed. So when he arrived a half hour later and his driver stayed in the car, I didn't know what to think.

"Come on in," I instructed, motioning Monty through the open doorway.

He glided into the foyer in a suit and tie, his leather shoes polished, his gray hair slicked back, and his brown eyes distant. I shut the front door and led him into the living room. There was a manila envelope tucked beneath his arm, and I didn't know what to make of it.

"The house is lovely as always, Finley."

"Thank you." I took a seat on the couch, but Monty seemed determined to stand.

"Finley," he addressed. "I'm afraid I have some very bad news."

All of my anxiety came brimming to the surface, as I watched him expectantly. My palms felt sweaty, yet my arms were cold. I didn't know how much more stress I could handle.

"There's no best way to say it, so here." Monty handed me the envelope, and then stood before the fireplace examining our stockings. "Open it," he directed with his back to me.

Forcing myself to swallow, I opened the flap and turned the mouth of the envelope upside down. Several full page printed photographs slid into my lap. But when I saw what the pictures were of, it shocked me how truly disappointed I was.

There must have been ten of them. Images of Cabel in bed with *her*. Jane. Dr. Adams. His ex-fiancé. His former classmate. His current mistress.

"I didn't know how to tell you this, Finley, but I thought you had a right to know." He waited a beat before adding, "I'm so sorry."

Holding my chin up, I maintained a straight face and set the pictures aside. While Monty had spared me from seeing their naked bodies together, I had just seen Jane in a bra. And Cabel beneath the sheets with her. That was enough.

"I already know."

"You already know?" Monty questioned.

"Yeah. I've been suspicious for a while."

"Finley, I don't know what to say. I never had children, but Cabel has always been like a son to me. Even before Blain and I got into politics. When Cabel was a child, Blain used to torture him. I always tried to stick up for the kid. But—"

"You don't have to tell me all that, Monty." I stood up and felt shaky. "Not right now."

"Okay." He stood by the fire with his hands folded behind his back.

"Who took these pictures?" I asked without making eye contact. "These photos of them together?"

"Well you know I've kept tabs on the two of you for security reasons."

"Yes, I know."

"It's always just been for your protection. But this time, I guess it was personal."

"What do you mean?" I gazed up at him, forgetting the photos on the couch beside me.

"I'll protect Cabel, but not over something like this." He sat down beside me and took my hand. "You deserve better."

Still in a state of shock, I stared at the fire, watching the flames wither and grow. I must have been in denial, because it was all too much. I could hardly see.

"I'm pregnant," I croaked.

"What?" Monty rose from the couch and set his hands on his hips.

"I'm pregnant," I repeated. "I just found out. Yesterday, actually. I went to Cabel's office to tell him, but he was with her."

Monty shook his head and sighed.

"Do you remember me telling you that you weren't right for each other?"

"That's what you meant?"

He lifted his eyebrows and shrugged.

"You knew him back then," I remembered. "So you must know Jane. How long were they together?"

"Two years."

Two years. We hadn't even been married that

long.

"Why did they end it?"

"I don't know," Monty revealed. "He wouldn't say."

Nodding, I held myself together for the time being. Within Monty's presence, I could keep my cool. But after he left...

"What am I supposed to do?"

"Talk to him." Monty patted my knee in reassurance, but it hardly helped.

"Why didn't you warn me?" I accused, widening my big brown eyes at him.

"I did. But face it kid, you were going to do what you wanted anyway. You love him. Back then. Maybe even now. Still."

"Yes," I whispered, shedding the first of my tears since Monty had arrived. "I do."

Monty wrapped his arm around me, and it seemed like lately I had been crying into everyone's shirt but my husband's. Even Jeremy's.

"Shh." Monty rubbed my back and handed me a handkerchief. I didn't even know men still carried these nowadays. "It's all right."

"I don't know what to do."

Monty tucked a fallen lock behind my ear and turned my chin up in the palm of his hand. "Give yourself some time to think. But you need to talk to Cabel."

"I know," I muttered.

Beyond exhausted, I gave Monty a hug and sat back on the couch. "I think I need to be alone."

"I understand." Monty left me his handkerchief, as well as the photos, and then left the room.

I followed him to the front door, wanting to tell him thank you. Thank you for telling me. Thank you for comforting me. Thank you for enlightening me. But I couldn't, because I didn't feel thankful.

"If you need to get away, you can always come stay with me for a while. I'm never there, with all the traveling. It's a big house, and you're welcome to use it whenever you like."

"Okay."

Monty kissed me on the cheek and then stepped through the open door. "By the way, I'm in town until tomorrow. Let me know if you need anything."

With a slight nod, I dried my eyes and shut the door. When his driver pulled away, I gave in to a complete breakdown on the floor. By the time I managed to get up again, I returned to the living room and looked at those pictures again. Feeling sick, I ran into the bathroom to vomit. When I was done, I didn't know what I was going to do.

My husband was having an affair, and I was pregnant with his child.

Chapter 12

When Cabel came home that night, I was upstairs packing, though not for our trip. The trip that was never going to happen. The closest thing that we would ever have to a honeymoon would be a day in court with two lawyers and a judge.

It surprised me when Cabel didn't come upstairs to even acknowledge my presence in the house. Though I shouldn't have been surprised, really. After flipping through those photos until I couldn't stand to look at them anymore, I had shut myself up in the closet and wept like a newly minted widow. Because that's what Cabel was to me. Dead.

Monty had been right all along, and how I wished that I had listened to him back then. He knew Cabel better than me. As it turns out, I didn't know him at all.

Once I had packed enough to survive without him, I got dressed and brushed my teeth. For the rest of the year, I would have to suck it up and be strong. Monty was taking me away from here, where Cabel couldn't hurt me anymore.

Downstairs, I found Cabel in his office, so I knocked on one of the French doors. He saw me through the glass and gestured his hand in my direction. "Come in, Mrs. Jones."

Bracing myself, I took a deep breath and stepped inside. Cabel sat at the computer, finalizing grades or checking exams or whatever he was doing. I didn't care anymore.

"So I'm guessing you're still mad at me." His ice blue eyes flitted up to meet mine, and I wished I'd never seen them before.

Although I wanted to be that woman, the one who threw the photographs in his face and stormed off, I couldn't. I didn't have enough energy to. So I kept my cool, out of respect for Cabel as another person, one human being to another.

I felt Cabel's eyes on me as I stepped forward, refusing to look at him, and set the stack of photos on his desk.

"I want a divorce," I numbly stated.

Cabel hardly had time to thumb through the photos before he stared up at me, eyes wide.

"I—but," he stuttered, riffling through the rest of the pictures. "Where did you get these?"

"Does it matter?" I felt very cold and couldn't wait for Monty to arrive.

"Finley." He rose from his seat in one abrupt motion. "I didn't do it. I didn't do this."

My eyes were drifting his way, but I shot them down to the floor. I couldn't bear to look at him.

Not because of what he did or how he had hurt me. But because I was still in love with him. I would always love him. And that stung harder than any knife in the chest.

"Finley, baby," he cooed. "You've got to believe me." He took a step closer, and I backed away. "I would never cheat on you."

Withholding my tears, I turned on my heel and walked away. "We can discuss this later."

Cabel followed me into the foyer, and I heard his audible gasp at the sight of my suitcase by the door.

"You're leaving me?" He snatched my elbow and twisted me back into his arms. "You can't! Not like this. I haven't even done anything."

The levy broke, and I started to cry. When he placed my head on his chest, I didn't pull away. I let him stroke his fingers through my hair and call me "baby."

Cabel was all I had ever wanted. And despite his flaws as a human, he had been perfect to me. But he wasn't my golden boy anymore. He had found himself a perfect golden girl to replace me.

"Finley, I don't know who took those pictures, but that's not me. It can't be! I've been with no one but you."

"Stop it!" I screamed, withdrawing from his grasp. "Stop lying to me! Just stop," I cried, leaning into the door.

When I crumpled to the floor, Cabel knelt down beside me and took my face in his hands. I had missed his touch, but it wasn't mine anymore. Cabel belonged to Jane.

"Finley, I didn't do this. Please believe me," he begged.

"I can't!"

He dropped his hands, and we sat there staring at each other for the longest time. Eventually, he said, "How can you do this to me, Finley? You're my whole life, my whole world. I'll never forgive you if you just—"

I smacked Cabel across the face so hard that my hand stung like fire. He rocked back on his heels and touched his cheek, in awe that I had slapped him.

"Can't you just tell me the truth?" I whimpered. "You've already hurt me enough. Don't I deserve that much?"

Cabel stood up and scowled.

"I have been telling you the truth, but you won't believe it."

"How can I when there are pictures of you with her? Explain those to me! What am I supposed to believe? That you've been having an affair without even knowing it?"

"I'm not having an affair!" he shouted, towering over me.

Eyeing him like the lying, cheating adulterer that he was, I wrapped my arms around myself and poked at my ribs with my finger. So this was who I had married, someone who would deny it to the grave. How had I ever believed anything that came out of his mouth?

"I've been nothing but honest with you," he defended. "Sure, I didn't tell you who Jane was at first. But I'm not a cheater, Finley." He rubbed his hands over his face and stopped before the staircase, leaning on the banister. "What kills me is that you won't believe me!"

Feeling small, I tucked my knees into my chest and stared at the hardwood floors. My mind traveled back in time, to when I had first seen this house, one I had thought that I would always be able to call home. But this wasn't home anymore. It was the epitome of betrayal.

"If you saw pictures of me in bed with another man, and I told you that it was all a lie, you're telling me that you would believe me?"

Cabel ground his teeth together, then set his hands on his hips. When he started pacing, I knew that I had him pegged.

"You're a liar," I declared. "I can't believe that for a while there, I actually thought you loved me."

"But I do love you!" Cabel cried, his booming voice echoing through the house.

I gazed up at him, and there were heavy tears in his crystal blue eyes. Though the sight of them ripped my heart to shreds, I couldn't bear to be in his presence any longer. If I was lucky, I would never have to see him again.

"If you love me, then you'll let me go," I said, my lower lip quivering.

"But I don't want to let you go," he sobbed.

Tired of living in this nightmare, I gathered myself up enough to stand on two feet and then reached for my luggage. At the sight, Cabel collapsed at my feet and stood on his knees. He clung to my legs and placed his head on my stomach, hugging me close. When his arms went around my waist, he was squeezing so tightly that I could barely breathe.

"Cabel," I wheezed, feeling the pressure in my ribs. "Stop, you're hurting me."

He withdrew immediately and gazed into my eyes like a wounded puppy.

"I'm sorry," he said.

Shaking my head in disgust, I grabbed my bags and opened the door. Relief flooded through me when I saw a black Mercedes SUV parked outside. Monty was here.

"Finley," Cabel gasped, wrapping his hand around my arm. "Don't go. Please, baby. I'm begging you."

Trying my best to look at him one last time with pleasant regard, I pressed my lips together and inhaled. "Monty is taking me to his house. He'll be traveling all the time, so he's offered to let me stay. I'll call you when I get there, just to let you know I'm safe."

Cabel's mouth dropped wide open before I even finished speaking. "Monty?" He looked past my shoulder and saw the SUV in the drive. "Finley, don't go with him," he commanded.

"Why?" I snapped my head back, angry that

he thought he had a right to tell me what to do. "You honestly think I'd rather stay here with you?"

I turned on my heel, and Cabel clutched my elbow in one firm grip. "I'm warning you, Finley. Don't get in that car with Monty. Something's not right."

Glowering up at him, I saw through the warm tears in my eyes and growled, "Take your hands off me."

In the quietest moment, Cabel let me go. I scanned him from head to toe, entirely consumed with outrage and disappointment. How had I ever fallen for him?

"Don't follow me." I forced Cabel back into the house and shut the front door, swiftly locking it behind me. As I scurried over to the SUV, I thought I heard the sound of glass shattering inside. I hurried my footsteps and ignored the noises. Perhaps Cabel couldn't handle the realization that I was actually leaving him.

Overhearing the commotion, Monty stepped out of the backseat and grabbed my luggage to stow away in the trunk. The windows were tinted, so I assumed security was sitting up front, with Monty running for office and all.

"You can sit back here with me," Monty offered, slamming the trunk.

I slid into the backseat, as Monty hopped in right behind me. The scent of lemon and leather filled my nostrils, alluding to that new car smell.

Monty shut the door and the driver took off. It was only then that I realized it was just us three.

Suddenly, the car stopped, and the driver removed a black wig and matching hat. She turned back to me and smiled. Immediately, I knew that Cabel's instincts had been right. Something was terribly wrong.

"Finley," Monty chirped. "Meet my daughter, Jane."

Chapter 13

I broke out in a sweat and reached for the door handle, but it was locked. All of my instincts were telling me to run, but I couldn't. I was trapped.

"Monty, what's going on?" I watched Jane smile and nearly burst into tears.

"I'm sorry, kid. But you simply know too much."

"Too much about what?" I grasped the side of the door, feeling my insides churning.

"My past, Cabel, Blain."

My eyes darted from left to right, as I tried to keep from falling apart.

"Monty." I licked my lower lip, each breath coming out harsh and ragged. "I swore to you that I would never say a word. Don't you believe me?"

Monty stroked my chin with his fingers. "Of course."

"But, but why?"

The door to the house slammed open, and two men dragged Cabel out kicking and screaming.

"Finley!" he shouted.

"What's going on? What are they doing to

him?"

No one answered me, so I leapt across the backseat and banged on the window.

"Cabel! CABEL!" I screeched, beating my fists against the glass even though it hurt.

The men took him off into the woods, through the trees, and I felt my blood turn cold.

"What's going on?" I repeated, though my voice was no louder than a whisper.

"Do you remember these?" Jane tossed a pile of photos at me, but she wasn't in them. They were the ones of Cabel and me. When I was his student, and we had run away together in the wilderness.

"It was you?" I breathed.

"Yes. To let you know that someone was watching. Only then it occurred to me that I would need to do more than get him fired." She reached into the glove compartment and handed me another set of photos. The ones of her and Cabel.

I hardly glanced at them before she spoke up again.

"So then I had to use these."

Unlike the copies I had been given, these originals had dates. In my head, I calculated that these had been taken at Cornell, when they were both in grad school. For the first time, I also noticed that the scar on Cabel's arm, where he had been shot, was missing.

"Why do you have these pictures?" I asked, my eyes still wandering over each of them. I couldn't believe that I hadn't noticed it before, but Cabel did look a lot younger here.

"I take pictures of all my boyfriends. Just in case I need something from them later."

"You blackmail them?"

"Sometimes. But I doubt Cabel remembers that night. He was practically unconscious." When my eyes widened, she went on. "He was calling off our engagement. So I just slipped something into his drink at dinner."

Realizing my deadly mistake, I set both sets of photos down, and the wheels were turning inside my head. Everything around me seemed to be spinning, and there was a thrumming pulse in my ears. I wanted to vomit.

"So I guess this means..."

"No, Cabel never cheated on you. Trust me, I tried, but I guess he really loves you. I don't think he ever felt that way about me."

Succumbing to my emotions, I started wailing and threw the pictures at Monty until they scattered across his lap.

"Why?" I demanded.

"Because the two of you are weaker apart. It was the only way to get you alone. The only way to get you to come willingly."

"And you bought into us so easily," Jane added. "Hook, line, and sinker."

I shook my head, wishing it all away, wanting it to be a bad dream.

"I thought you didn't have children," I told

Monty.

"She's a love child from my past."

"And you're not going to ruin his future," Jane snipped. "Besides, Cabel was mine first. It's only natural that I should hate you."

So here was the heart of the matter. A bitter ex who wanted to see her replacement suffer. And a ruthless politician who was nothing more than a clone of Blain Ulrich. He was clearing all the skeletons out of his closet. Just like someone else had a few years ago.

"It's simple, really," Monty claimed. "You saw something that you weren't supposed to see."

I remembered Ulrich essentially telling me the exact same thing. But when Monty had let us go, I never realized he would be watching us, plotting against us, waiting for the perfect opportunity to tear us apart. He wanted to eliminate the threat of all that we had been keeping secret.

Monty had murdered the promising headliner intended to become the next presidential candidate. And while I had believed that Blain would have killed Cabel, had Monty not stepped in the way, I was starting to wonder if his motives went beyond the realm of self-defense. Maybe he had simply been weeding out his competition.

"You're going to kill me. Aren't you?"

Monty gazed out the window, avoiding my question.

"No." Jane turned towards me from the front seat at an angle. "We're going to kill Cabel. And you're going to watch."

She lunged forward and hit me in the face, then threw a bag over my head. Within seconds, I was in the black, no longer seeing stars.

Chapter 14

When I roused awake, my hands were tied, and I was lying in the trunk of a moving car. As my eyes adjusted to the darkness, I found Cabel stretched out beside me. He wasn't moving, and I worried that maybe I had blocked it from my mind. Maybe they had already done it.

"Cabel," I hissed, unable to move my arms, because of the rope around my wrists.

Before I would give up so easily, I inched closer and clamped my teeth around his ear. When I bit down, hoping that he would feel it, Cabel flinched in pain and opened his eyes.

"Baby," I whispered, relieved that he was still alive.

He grunted and exhaled aloud.

"Baby, I'm so sorry. They're going to kill us, and it's all my fault."

"No, it's not," he muttered. "If I had it to go all over again, I wouldn't change a thing."

Tears dripped down from my eyes, as I felt his breath on my face. It was like a healing balm, because that meant he was closer.

"Cabel, I'm sorry," I cried. "I'm so, so sorry

that I didn't believe you."

"It's okay. I'm just glad you know the truth."

The car stopped, and my heart nearly exploded out of my chest. Was this it? Was this all we were going to get?

"Cabel," I panicked, squirming around in the trunk.

"Don't be scared," he advised.

I had never heard him talk so calmly in a situation like this. He wasn't being sensible.

The trunk popped open as the cool night air and moonlight rained down on us. The two men who had taken Cabel off to the woods jerked each of us to our feet. Jane and Monty were standing in front of the SUV parked beside us. I was surprised that neither had a gun in their hand.

With my hands tied behind my back, I couldn't do much more than walk where the man told me. At the sound of crushing waves, I reared back. But the man steered me farther to the edge of the cliff made of rocks. It was a steep drop down to the ocean below.

They taped my mouth and tied rope around my ankles before attaching a concrete block. My anchor, my weight, the heavy object to send me sinking down, down, down to the deepest part of the ocean.

When the man finished preparing for my demise, Cabel became more alert, fighting and bucking against Monty's other henchman, who held him back. Cabel elbowed the man in the jaw when he tried to put tape over his mouth. But then Jane kicked Cabel in the back, and he staggered forward on the ground. She grabbed his hair and pulled, forcing him to tilt his head back.

"Please," he rasped. "I'll do whatever you want. Just let her live."

Jane took his face in her hands and kissed him to spite me, smearing red lipstick at the corner of his mouth. Then she grabbed a roll of tape to force his lips shut, and Monty nodded to the man holding me captive.

"NO! DON'T!" Cabel screamed, falling to the ground face first, for he had no way of using his hands to brace himself. "She's pregnant!"

I looked over at Cabel with shock, though Monty did not care for his pleas. Instead, his eyes flitted from mine to Cabel's. They were so devoid of emotion that he almost looked unrecognizable.

"I know," Monty responded.

Then he gestured my way, and I was pushed off the edge, scraping the cliff rocks as the concrete block tied to my ankles jerked me forward. Falling felt like an amusement park ride, pounding and pulsing excitement and fear to my core. But then I broke the plane of what felt like a sheet of ice, and suddenly, I wasn't falling anymore.

Part II
The Lonely Boy

Chapter 15

My body was freezing, shivering, shuddering. I felt myself traveling to a midway point between petrified and scared, not knowing if I would feel more pain alive or dead. Something cloaked around me, draping my shoulders with warmth.

Fighting the urge to sleep, I was desperate to force my eyes open, but they seemed to be sealed shut. I was trapped inside of a bad dream, the kind where a momentary bout of paralysis takes over, the kind where you aren't able to wake up. The stinging cold felt like a memory, but with every flutter of my lashes, I knew that it wasn't.

For hours I drifted in and out of this "death sleep," not knowing if an angel was coming to take me to heaven, or if a demon cast from hell had arrived on earth to torture me.

Somehow, in the deepest crevice of my mind, I knew that it wasn't just me anymore. The body I had inhabited for twenty-two years was now occupied with a growing infant.

A child. My child. *His* child.

The image of Cabel flickered to mind, while I

wrestled with my own state of consciousness. His shiny blonde hair looked gloriously golden in the light, his piercing blue eyes sharp and cool blue enough to catch anyone's attention across a crowded room. He was so beautiful, and I knew that the image I had conjured of him in my mind wasn't laced with worry or longing or regret. It was a picture of him from my memory, when I had been a shy teenager, out in the rain. A modern day damsel in distress.

"Finley," a sweet voice called, sounding so much like an angel's that I wondered if I had reached the afterlife yet. Had he been taken, too?

The touch of a warm hand to my shoulder left my skin singing at the caress. I felt myself being pulled towards the sensation, and the person who had touched me. It was an uphill battle, my attempt to will myself awake. When my eyes finally opened, it was like peeling back the curtains on a sunny day, but he was there. He had not left me, and in that moment, I knew he never would.

He was all the light I would ever need.

"Finley," he gasped with relief.

As I took in my new surroundings, my heart lurched inside of my chest. I was lying on a bed wrapped in white linen sheets and warm cotton blankets. In time, I came to understand that we were in the master bedroom of a hotel suite, with a high rise view overlooking the ocean. Realizing the awful nightmare, I closed my eyes and sighed. Cabel and I were on our honeymoon, the one we had yet to take, and everything else had been a bad dream.

"Baby?" Cabel called, squeezing my hand. He felt so warm, and I didn't want to let go.

Wondering what that terrible noise was, I realized that I was trembling, because my own teeth were clacking together. In an instant, I recognized the pain in my head, a throbbing discomfort, not unlike the ache in my ribs. Truthfully, I ached all over, and even the back of my throat felt sore.

"I'm c-c-c-cold," I announced with chattering teeth. Despite the plethora of covers cocooning my body, all I felt was freezing.

When Cabel pulled the covers back, it felt like ripping off a Band-Aid, and I shuddered. Shutting my eyes, I encircled my waist with my arms, hugging my own body to create some kind of warmth. The sound of Cabel unbuckling his belt caused me to glimpse at him through the thin slits of my partially closed eyelids. After he took his shirt off and tossed it aside, Cabel knelt down on the bed and began tugging my clothes off.

"No," I resisted, though my body was much too weak to keep him away.

Cabel ignored me and stripped my clothes off, my whole body shaking in response. I squeezed my eyes shut and cradled my elbows in the palm of each hand, curling my knees into my stomach. But then I felt two hands of fire slide around my waist, and Cabel cuddled against my body beneath the covers.

He inhaled sharply, as I sank into the heat of his body, resting my head on his chest. I lay there in the warmth of his arms, clinging to him tightly, thawing the frostiness out of my skin. His hand went around my bare back, his fingers splayed out over my spine, as I let myself acclimate to the comforting sensation, the subtle transition from cold to hot.

I seemed to have no grasp on time, just the beating rhythm of Cabel's heart. Eventually, my ice cold skin warmed up, soon gathering a slight layer of perspiration from the amount of body heat. But I wasn't moving a muscle. I would rather lie here and sweat than risk being frozen again.

Cabel placed the back of his hand to my forehead, touching my dewy skin. Then he slipped a loose strand of hair behind my ear and gently traced a line from the end of my jaw to my chin. My lips parted in response, as I lifted my face to gaze at him.

"What happened?" I mouthed.

Cabel looked away, so I held his wrist and willed him to return his eyes to mine.

"They're gone," he coaxed, running his knuckles over my cheek. "We're safe now."

I furrowed my brow and leaned my head back into the pillow to get a better look at him. "Who's gone?"

Cabel blinked several times. "Monty and Jane. Don't you remember?"

So then it wasn't a dream.
"You nearly drowned."

Chapter 16

A harsh scream bolted from my lungs when I dropped into the stinging chill of the ocean. The tape over my mouth muted the sound, as I felt myself sinking lower, lower, lower. My feet ached with the pull of the block that was tied to my ankles.

I opened my eyes under the water and lifted my head to watch the surface level that I was drifting farther and farther away from. My lungs began to burn with fire, as I flailed around like an ungraceful mermaid, my arms and legs bound by rope. Panicking on the inside, I let the concrete drive me to the ocean floor, where my doom and death awaited me.

But then everything turned black. Right before it pulled me under, I could have sworn I caught a glimpse of my golden boy.

The next thing I remembered was Cabel's lips on my mouth, before I sat up and coughed all of the sea water up that I had inhaled through my nose. I could feel where he had ripped the tape away, because the skin above my lips felt chapped.

We must have hidden out in a cave, because in

my head I saw a room with walls and a ceiling made of rock. I faintly recalled a fire, whose flames Cabel had used to burn the rope around my ankles and wrists. Even now, the cold stone floor of the cave felt like an ever-present memory. So how had we ended up here?

* * *

Widening my eyes at the realization, I glanced down at my wrists to find evidence based on the impression marks in my skin. I looked through the window that stretched from ceiling to floor and watched the tumbling waves of the sea. The same sea that had nearly killed me.

"We have to get out of here," I demanded, my pulse quickening hot and hard. "They'll find us."

I heard someone knocking in the distance and flinched, my eyes widening with terror.

"It's just room service," Cabel assured me. "I already told them to leave it outside the door."

My breathing increased, but he held a hand up in the air, a gesture to encourage me to calm down.

"I'll be right back." Cabel left me in bed and walked into the adjoining room.

I held my breath and pressed my lips together until he came back. When he returned, he was steering a metal cart in my direction. He had ordered a plate of grilled chicken with rice and vegetables, as well as a bowl of soup.

Cabel turned to reach for something out of a

plastic bag in the chair by the window. From the wording on the front of it, I gathered that Cabel had picked up some clothes, probably from a shop in the hotel lobby. He fished a t-shirt out and tossed it across the bed at me.

I pulled the soft cotton garment over my head and let Cabel set the tray of food in my lap. Even though the shirt was much too large, fitting more like a dress, it was extremely comfortable. As he sat down on the edge of the mattress, I intended to take my plate and hand it to him, but he shook his head at me.

"I already ate," he explained. "Earlier. When you were sleeping."

I sat there for a moment, too in shock to move, so I fell silent.

"Finley, you need to eat," he ordered. "It's not just you anymore."

Picking up a silver fork, I took a few bites of the rice, and my hunger resurfaced. Despite the soreness in my throat, I swallowed most of the vegetables without much chewing at all. The baby was starving, and so was I.

"How did you know?" I cut a piece of grilled chicken and popped it into my mouth. "About the baby?"

Cabel exhaled and stroked the light stubble on his face. "The doctor's office called. Something about setting up an appointment with an OBGYN."

I chewed and swallowed.

"And you left a pamphlet on the counter in the kitchen."

That must have been the information the doctor had given me the other day, including the list of acceptable foods to eat.

"Why didn't you tell me you knew?" I asked.

Cabel looked at me and glared. "I don't know. Maybe I was waiting for you to tell me."

Stung by his sarcasm, I placed my empty tray back on the cart. Though I might have eaten too quickly, I felt immediate relief in my stomach. It was nice to be full.

"I was going to tell you," I confessed. "I drove straight to your office as soon as I found out, but you were—" I broke off, averting my gaze. "You were in there with Jane."

Cabel nodded, but I noticed the way he was clenching his jaw. I recognized that deep smolder. He was mad.

"You were really just going to leave? Without telling me that you were pregnant with my child?"

"Well, I didn't think you would care," I argued. "I thought you were cheating on me with Jane! How did you expect me to feel?"

Cabel leaned in and lowered his voice. "I expected you to believe me."

Swallowing, I exhaled through my nostrils and tugged the covers up to my waist.

"Well, I'm sorry."

"Sorry doesn't cut it, Finley." He stood up and headed towards the bathroom. "You've broken my trust. And if you can't trust me, then I don't think I can trust you either."

"Cabel."

He stepped inside the bathroom and shut the door behind him. When I heard it lock, that sound cut like a knife. Then the shower came on, as I lay down beneath the covers. It seemed that our relationship was going to need some rebuilding.

Anxious and bored, I spotted a remote control on the bedside table and picked it up. There was a TV on the dresser directly across from the foot of the bed. Pressing the power button, I watched the screen light up, and it took all I could not to scream.

Monty was on TV.

Chapter 17

By the time Cabel got out of the shower and came into the bedroom with a towel around his waist, Monty had nearly finished the press conference. He looked sharp as a tack in a freshly pressed suit, nothing like the man I had encountered earlier. Then again, it had become clear to me that Monty got others to do his dirty work for him.

Throughout the course of his speech, I noticed how familiar his way of addressing an audience was. He even used phrases that must have been taken right out of Blain Ulrich's mouth. Regardless, the TV appearance did calm my nerves in one regard. It meant that Monty and everyone connected with him were very far away from here.

"He thinks we're dead," Cabel announced.

I sat back against the headboard and read the location of the press conference at the bottom of the screen. Monty must have boarded a plane and flown straight there, because he was several states away from us. When he walked off the stage, I realized why he had held a public speaking event at the last minute.

To secure an alibi.

Cabel took the remote and clicked the TV off, then pulled on a shirt and a pair of sweatpants.

"This is good," Cabel noted, closing the curtains. "This means he doesn't know we're here. He doesn't know we're still alive."

"And what about when he finds out that we are?"

Cabel made eye contact with me and moved closer, setting his hands on the bed and holding his face before mine. I moistened my lips and felt an increase in my heart rate. Even though we had been at war with each other for the past couple of days, it felt like it had been so long since he had touched me.

"He's not going to."

Cabel scanned the length of my figure, then took a cautious step back. When he walked around to the other side of the bed and grabbed his pillow, I huffed aloud. He looked over at me and then made for the other room.

"Cabel," I whined. "Where are you going?"

"To sleep on the couch," he grunted, slamming the bedroom door behind him.

Igniting with rage, I climbed out of bed and stormed into the adjoining room. There was a full kitchen to the left with a corresponding table and living room to the right. Cabel was sprawled out on the couch without so much as a blanket for cover.

"What do you think you're doing?"

Cabel lifted his head in surprise, not expecting the tone I had taken with him. But then his eyes darkened, and he turned on the TV with the remote in his hand. While he lay there and ignored me, I balled my hands into fists at my sides. I knew what I wanted, and this was not it.

"Last time I checked, you wanted a divorce," Cabel reminded me.

"That's because I thought you were cheating on me!"

Cabel sat up on the couch, obviously annoyed with me already. "And when I told you that I wasn't, you didn't believe me!"

I twisted my fingers through my hair and stomped my foot on the ground. "That's because they lied to me. Monty and Jane messed with my head and made me think that you were someone that you're not."

"But if you knew me well enough, shouldn't you have been able to see that they were lying?" Cabel stood up and breathed down my face. "The only reason you believed them is because you don't trust me."

I took a step back, and the back of my knees butted up against the coffee table in front of the sofa. "Cabel, I–I..." Words abandoned me, because what he had said was true. If I really trusted Cabel, I would have believed no one but him.

"I'm sorry," I coaxed.

"You've been punishing me for something I

didn't even do. You didn't even tell me that you were pregnant. How do you think that makes me feel?"

"Cabel—"

He cut me off and marched into the kitchen, fetching a glass of water from the sink. After draining the glass dry, he set it down on the counter and wiped his mouth with the tail of his shirt. I caught a glimpse of his abs before he pulled the garment back down, and it seemed like he had done it just to tease me.

"Unless it's someone else's," he accused.

My frustration turned to rage. "What?" I snapped, my eye twitching in the process. For a moment, he truly looked scared, as I cornered him by the fridge. "What did you just say to me?"

"Maybe you're the one who's been seeing someone else," he suggested. "Maybe that's why you were in such a hurry to leave and divorce me."

My eyes watered with tears, and I hated them for betraying me. I wasn't sad. I was angry.

"It doesn't feel so good now. Does it?" Cabel kept his eyes on me, and I could see what he was trying to do.

I turned away from him and pressed my palms into the countertop to keep myself steady. "Did you know Monty had a daughter?"

"No," he answered. "I've always been under the impression that Monty never had kids."

"So have I," I meekly stated. There was a burning sensation in my chest, and it was spreading elsewhere.

"Jane always told me that she never met her father. Trust me. I'm just as shocked as you are."

A moment of silence passed between us, and I couldn't stand the feeling that it was an accurate reflection of our relationship at present. Despite the strange and dangerous circumstances, the past twenty-four hours had tested our faith in each other. I wondered if Cabel still trusted me.

"Why didn't you believe me?" Cabel piped up in the quiet. The hairs were standing up on the back of my neck, and I knew he was hovering behind me.

"Because Jane seemed perfect. Tall. Blonde. Beautiful. Already a professor. Your age. Everything that I'm not. How could I compete with that?"

Cabel placed his hands on my shoulders, as my entire body thrummed with delight. Whenever he touched me, I wanted the sensation to last a lifetime. Now that I was pregnant, carrying his child, there was something different about the way he made me feel.

"You don't know how good you are."

"What?" I took a breath at his words, unable to understand the meaning in them.

Cabel turned me around to face him and gently held my arms. His eyes followed my line of sight, and I enjoyed the way his perpetual gaze fell on my face.

"I've been waiting my whole life to meet

somebody like you," he confessed.

"I don't understand."

Our eyes met, and I could hardly find the blue in his. They were dark, brooding, filled with desire. I knew my own eyes must have been dilating just the same.

He lifted his hand to my face. "You're good, pure, innocent. And by some miracle, you're mine."

I gazed up at him and felt a shudder run through my voice. "Everyone thinks I'm just some student who slept her way to the top. Jane said that's the only reason I made it into the graduate program, because I'm your wife."

"And why would you listen to her?" he countered.

"Like you have room to talk," I bit back. "Those pictures were from the night you broke off the engagement by the way."

Cabel clenched his jaw and glared.

"She put something in your drink."

When he started pacing, I turned on my heel. But Cabel grabbed ahold of my elbow and pulled me back. "We're not done talking," he commanded.

"About what? Jane?" I jabbed. "Are there any other ex-girlfriends I should know about?"

Cabel released my arm and let me go, the wound marks I had left visible in the etched planes of anxiety on his face. Now that I looked back, we had gotten married so fast. And at the time, we hadn't spoken in two years. Maybe we really didn't know each other at all.

"I always hoped you'd come back to me, Finley. I just never thought you actually would."

Seeing the sadness in his eyes, I thought about all the misery we had gone through, the tortuous agony of having to wait to be together. How could I just let Jane waltz in and destroy everything? I was the one who had allowed her to manipulate the situation and leave my own husband when he hadn't even done anything wrong. If there were any bruises on his heart, they were my doing. It was my duty to mend every broken promise until they were all fixed.

"I'm sorry," I uttered.

Cabel immediately lifted his head at the sound of my words, as stunned as he was pleased. He looked tired. He looked damaged. He looked heartbroken.

"I'm sorry." My tears returned, and I was about to walk away when Cabel tugged at my elbow. He shortened the distance between us, his nostrils flaring as I came closer. Then he studied my mouth and sank his teeth into his lower lip. I didn't need any more of an apology.

"I want you," he breathed.

I inhaled and swallowed, captured beneath his seductive spell.

"Ever since the first time I saw you standing there in the rain."

"Cabel," I cried out in longing, as he mercifully

crushed his lips to mine.

My arms circled around the back of his neck, and I pulled him closer to me. Cabel groaned, fisting his hands in my hair like I had been denying him for centuries. I leaned forward on the tips of my toes and nearly lost my balance until he caught my weak body and carried me to the couch. It was much closer than the bed.

Chapter 18

Yet somehow, we ended up there anyway. I stretched out on my front, adoring the soft texture of the mattress beneath me. Cabel lay on the other side of the bed, pushing fallen locks out of my face as I looked around the pillow at him. There was an adorable smile on his face, a crooked one that lifted his mouth at the corner.

"My back hurts," I murmured. It had been aching ever since I stirred awake, just like every other part of my body, but I hadn't thought to complain until now.

Cabel took the hint and cocked his head to the side. Satisfaction flitted over his features, because he wanted to take care of me.

I turned the side of my face into the pillow, fighting to keep my eyes open. He set his hands on the bare skin of my shoulder blades and began rubbing my back. Letting my eyes shut in contentment, I stretched my legs out and sighed.

Cabel slid his thumb along my spine, his fingers kneading my flesh. When he wrapped his hands around my shoulders and squeezed, I felt my eyelids flutter. Then he dragged his nails along the surface of my back, and my skin had never felt so sensitive.

"What are we doing here?" I mumbled, though my stress level was waning.

"What do you mean?" Cabel traced circular patterns over my neck, his fingertips digging into my bare skin.

"We're staying at a hotel," I softly spoke. "That's not exactly inconspicuous."

Cabel stopped the massage and I groaned. Then he chuckled and returned his wonderful hands to my back. I tucked my arms beneath the pillow, unraveling at the feel of his gentle touch.

"I checked us in under a different name. Don't worry, we'll be fine."

"What name?" I wondered.

"Finley," he scolded. "Can't you just trust me for once? I know what I'm doing."

Rising up on my elbows, I looked him over and tried to disguise the fear in my eyes. I just couldn't see how this plan was going to work. Like a snake in the grass, Monty would rise up and strike. Even if we remained here unseen, we couldn't hide away forever. When the new semester began, how were either of us going to return to school and work? We couldn't simply resume living while Monty thought we were dead.

Cabel slipped his finger beneath my chin and gazed into my eyes. "I'm not gonna let anything happen to you." He traced his fingertips along the curves and lines of my face. "Either of you."

I sucked in a breath and sighed. It was more than just my life or Cabel's life now. I was afraid for the two of us, but nothing matched the terror I felt for our child.

Closing my eyes, I aimed to steady my breathing, but nothing left me feeling even remotely calm until Cabel pressed his lips to my neck. His kisses traveled to my shoulders and then down my back. I closed my eyes and relaxed, feeling his hand settle along my ribcage. Then his mouth reached my ear, and I made sure to listen.

"Turn over," he whispered, his breath a warm, teasing caress.

Intrigued, I did as he said and slowly rolled onto my back. He propped up beside me on his elbow, and my eyes became clear and alert. Cabel placed his hand on my waist and then lowered his head, planting a sweet kiss on my stomach.

I couldn't help grinning like a fool, and when he leaned down to press his ear to my belly, I laughed. "Cabel, you can't hear the baby yet. It's too soon." I stroked my fingers through his hair as he held me tight, hugging my stomach.

"When I found out you were pregnant, I wanted to tell you so bad, how happy it made me. But then you wouldn't say anything." He caressed my skin, and I felt the stubble of his beard against my belly. "And that day you walked in on me and Jane..."

I curled my fingers around the back of his head and let him have a moment to think. "Go on," I encouraged.

"I knew what you thought. And it killed me, because if I had seen you with someone else," he drifted off again. "And then you just wouldn't believe me."

"Cabel, I'm sorry," I said. "I've told you I was sorry."

"I know," he murmured, kissing my belly again. "I'm sorry, too."

He fell silent after that and stayed that way for a very long time. His head lay on my stomach, as I had the strange feeling that there was something he was not telling me. But I didn't want to pry, our bounds of trust still too fragile for that.

Eventually, Cabel sat up and turned out the light. All went dark and quiet in the room, though I could hear the waves crashing along the shoreline outside. While I lay there in the silence, Cabel reached out for me and took my face in his hands. I whimpered at the way his mouth captured mine, because his abrupt passion had taken me by surprise.

He pulled me into his body, as I felt one hand go around the small of my back and the other cup the side of my face. When he drew a line along my lower lip with the pad of his thumb, I gasped for air. But then he claimed my mouth again, and I wholly surrendered to the place he was taking me.

Chapter 19

The next morning, I woke up to the sound of Cabel cursing aloud in the bathroom. I pulled a long t-shirt over my head and trotted in there to see what the matter was. Cabel stood over the sink with white foam on his face and a razor in his hand. It was then that I noticed the dot of blood on his cheek. Cabel had cut himself.

"Hey," I murmured, creeping closer. "Are you okay?"

Cabel caught sight of me in the mirror and watched my reflection move closer. I placed my hand on his bare back and regarded his shirtless state. Together, we were sharing a pajama set designed for one from the gift shop in the hotel lobby. Cabel donned the bottoms, while I wore the matching top.

Cabel dipped his razor into the pool of hot water that had gathered in the sink. "Yeah, I'm fine. Just nicked myself is all."

Concerned, I walked around Cabel and lifted myself onto the countertop beside him. When he turned from the mirror to me, I rubbed his arm gently. "Allow me," I suggested.

Twisting his mouth to the side, Cabel eyed me carefully. He was mulling the matter over in his mind, though there was a gentle blue look of confidence in his eyes.

"What?" I harped, intending to hurry him along. "You don't trust me?"

After one of our many recent arguments, I knew he would have to give in. How could he accuse me of not trusting him while he was doing the same? It was a test, surely, that would determine his level of trust, as well as mine. Without a word, Cabel handed the razor over, and I slid down off the counter.

Triumphant, I pulled a bathroom chair up to the sink and patted the soft seat. "Sit," I declared, quirking my brow at him in a flirtatious manner.

Cabel couldn't hide his grin, as he obeyed my command and sat down. "You really like telling me what to do. Don't you?"

Smirking with delight, I leaned down over him and touched the blade to his unshaven cheek. I noticed a stiffness in Cabel's posture as he held his breath, bracing himself, squaring his shoulders, and setting his palms over his thighs. As I dragged the razor along the length of his beautiful face, my heart beat faster. I didn't want to hurt him and was scared that I might.

Once his cheekbones were delectably smooth, setting a glorious contrast to his attractive bone structure, I dunked the head of the razor into the pool of hot water in the sink. Before I could look back, Cabel's palm landed on my thigh, slowly climbing its way up.

Feeling my skin begin to tingle, I grabbed his wrist and said, "Trying to distract me?"

Cabel drew a quick inhale of breath through his parted lips, those dangerously alert eyes testing mine. When he smirked, a rush of heat overwhelmed me, and I knew that my cheeks were blushing scarlet. Determined to finish the task laid out before me, I heated the razor with warm water again, and then pressed the blade against his throat.

Cabel swallowed, though he appeared less stiff than earlier. His steady gaze left a burning trail of heat inside my body, scorching and simmering. He could have branded me with that look, and I would have done nothing but like it.

"Lean your head back," I instructed, tilting his chin in that direction.

Cabel groaned, and I watched the pulse point against his throat. The rise and fall of his chest proudly displayed his taut, muscular shape. I remembered comparing him to the likes of Brad Pitt, Paul Newman, and even Robert Redford in my teenage years. Now, I could see that I hadn't been wrong.

When I finished shaving the last bit of stubble along his jawline and left him unmarked, Cabel rinsed his face off in the sink, and then patted his freshly cut hide dry with a towel. Admiring my handy work, Cabel touched the edge of his chin, turning his head every which way before the mirror. Apart from the minor nick he had left by his own hand, Cabel's skin was flawless.

"What?" I challenged, standing beside him. "Surprised I didn't cut you?"

Cabel pursed his lips together and shook his head. "No."

"Well, when you've been shaving your legs for nearly a decade," I started.

Cabel pulled me in and folded his arms around the small of my back. "Does that mean it's my turn?"

"Cabel," I chastised, giggling as he pressed his forehead to mine.

He smoldered, and I felt his warm breath rush over me. When he kissed my lips, I did not hesitate to let my heart open wide as his untainted love came crashing in. Cabel nibbled at the edge of my mouth, while I grabbed ahold of his biceps to steady myself.

In that moment, I knew that he had me fooled. I would buy into this façade of a reality where it didn't matter if Monty thought we were dead when we were actually alive. I had faith in a fairytale that we could live in a conspicuous location inconspicuously. It was all a fantasy, but I wanted so much to believe that we were safe, that no one would ever find us here, that Cabel and I had escaped unseen.

But maybe I wasn't a complete fool. Maybe it was denial not naiveté. Maybe it was hope in the pipe dream that our life could return to the way it once was. Maybe I cared too much for our only child and didn't want to harm a growing infant with any more stress on my body. Either way, I succumbed to the fake world Cabel had created. And I let myself believe that none of it was too good to be true.

Cabel's fingers tangled through my hair, as his other hand slipped beneath my shirt and trailed the length of my naked back. Clinging to him, I clasped my hands together behind his neck and whimpered when he tugged at my bottom lip. Cabel groaned at the sound that left my parted lips and pushed me up against the wall.

My hands searched his torso, rubbing and caressing his skin. His chest. His abs. His ribs. When Cabel folded his hands through mine and then ripped the shirt over the top of my head, I couldn't believe that he was mine. How had I gotten so lucky?

Cabel placed his hands at my waist and hauled me into the bedroom, where we collapsed on the mattress together. He stretched out beside me and cradled my face in his hands, similar to the first time we had made love. I felt his lips against my neck, as his fingers traveled along the sides of my arms and then my neck and then my spine.

Right before that pivotal moment, that felt so much like freezing fire and burning ice, he left the softest kiss on my lips, and I knew he would be gentle. His frosty blue eyes gazed into mine, loving, caring, trusting. Since the day I met Cabel Jones, he had taken every part of me, but none that I hadn't already been willing to give. As he braided his fingers through mine and pushed the back of my hands into the mattress, I knew that I had made my choice.

If he was going to burn, then I would burn with him.

Chapter 20

By the time Christmas Eve arrived, I had grown so used to enjoying the fake world Cabel had created, that nothing else seemed to matter. For the past seven days, we had stayed in that one hotel room, wasting time and making love. We did everything together—ate, drank, slept, even refused to bathe without the other. So maybe we were joined at the hip, and maybe that wasn't the healthiest way to avoid being co-dependent.

But I didn't care.

The baby had tied us together in more ways than one, and I couldn't have imagined what that would feel like. There was a part of him growing inside of me. It wasn't biology. It was a miracle.

All my life, I had never known when I would become a mother or if I even wanted to be one. It was hard to picture yourself as a parent when there was no man in your life. But Cabel had appeared out of nowhere, and my life was the better for it.

As he relaxed on the bed beside me, I caught a glimpse of him out of the corner of my eye. Surely, marriage wasn't like this for everyone.

There was no way that most people could feel about each other the way I felt about him. It was out of the ordinary. We were the minority. And whatever passion and chemistry had fused together between us most definitely wasn't usual.

Cabel flipped channels with the television remote, until I squealed at the sight of *The I Love Lucy Christmas Special* that had just come on. He chuckled and turned the volume up before setting the remote control aside. My eyes widened with delight, because even though we were far away and had no Christmas tree, Cabel was the one who felt like home to me.

"You're like a little girl," he teased.

"Hey!" I lightly punched him in the arm and narrowed my eyes in his direction.

My words came out garbled, since I was stuffing my face with macaroni and cheese. Cabel had ordered a feast for our Christmas dinner, insisting that he wanted me to be full. Apart from the occasional morning sickness, so far pregnancy was shaping up to be pretty rewarding.

After a pulled pork sandwich and a generous helping of coleslaw, I set my dishes aside on the serving tray, and Cabel left the cart outside our door. When he returned, I lay down on my side and relaxed beneath the covers. Lucy and Ethel were making me laugh, and for the first time, that hotel suite kind of felt like home.

Once the Christmas Special was over, Cabel turned the TV off and climbed into bed beside me. Now that my hunger and the baby's had been satisfied, I could hardly keep my eyes open. Food had been my number one priority, but now that it had been met, all I wanted to do was sleep.

When all the lights went off, Cabel rested his head against my shoulder, his nose brushing my neck. I listened to him inhale, and my skin tingled as he tucked a lock of hair behind my ear. Then his hand slipped beneath my shirt to feel of my belly.

"Do you think it's a boy or a girl?" he whispered in the dark.

I opened my eyes and smiled, turning my head in his direction.

"I don't know, really. But I've been thinking of names," I confessed. "Just one name, actually. For a girl."

"Well let's hear it."

Fluttering my lashes, I placed my hand on his chest and felt the calm nature of his heartbeat. "Cayley," I announced. "Spelled C-A-Y-L-E-Y."

"Hmm," he considered.

"It's your name mixed with mine. Kind of like how this baby is just as much a part of you as it is of me."

As my eyes adjusted to the darkness, I admired Cabel's figure beside me. His fingertips glided over my stomach, while we both reckoned with the fact that we had created another human being. There would be three of us now, and maybe that was what we had needed all along to become a family.

"I like it," Cabel eventually said.

"You do not," I rebutted.

"I do," Cabel insisted. "Seriously. I think Cayley sounds perfect."

The back of my head sank into the soft center of the pillow as I prepared to rest. Pleased that he had accepted one of the first baby names to come to mind, I covered the hand Cabel had laid over my stomach with my palm. His skin was warm, and I knew that I had never been destined to carry anyone's child but his.

"What if it's a boy?" he wondered.

I looked up at the ceiling, content to lie here with him and talk in the night. "I don't know," I realized. "I haven't really thought of any boy names."

"Well, I guess it will have to be a girl then."

"Why?"

Cabel shifted beside me and stretched his arm out across my torso in a protective manner. "Because I really like Cayley."

My spirits lifted as I squirmed around until I was comfortable enough to close my eyes. Cabel pulled my back into his chest so he could keep his hand on my stomach while I slept. Before I drifted off, the sound of Cabel whispering in my ear lulled me to sleep.

"Cabel Jones. Finley Jones. Cayley Jones. Hmm..."

Whatever he was saying sounded like heaven

to me. So I relaxed within the warm comfort and strength of his embrace and dozed off to the aspiration of our happy little family.

Chapter 21

Despite the strange circumstances, Christmas Day didn't feel terribly odd. Compared to the amount of holidays I had spent in foster care, this was a definite upgrade. With my beautiful husband serving me breakfast in bed, I couldn't ask for more.

"Cover your eyes," he said once I finished the plentiful supply of bacon and eggs.

"What?" I cracked a grin at the sight of him.

"Finley," he warned.

"All right, fine." I shut my eyes and then held my hands over them, just in case he thought I was peeking. My ears perked up at the sound of him rustling what must have been tissue paper inside of a bag. I wasn't used to receiving gifts on Christmas, but for the first time in years, someone was making sure that I did. But then it occurred to me that I had nothing to give Cabel, and I felt bad.

"All right. You can open your eyes." Cabel tugged at my wrists until my hands fell away. Sitting on the mattress beside me was a brown paper bag from the hotel gift shop. "Merry Christmas, Finley."

I wanted to reach out for the bag but hesitated. "But I didn't get you anything. I mean, I did, but it's at the house."

He held a hand up in the air. "It's okay. I just wanted you to have something to open on Christmas morning."

The sweetness of his forward thinking brought tears to my eyes. With my hormones jumping up and down, it was to be expected. But when I leaned forward on the bed and wrapped my arms around him, Cabel was surprised.

"Hey, baby," he cooed.

My chin went over his shoulder as I squeezed him tight, hardly able to control my own emotions. When I pulled back and he cradled my face in the palm of his hand, looking deep into my eyes, I took a breath and pounced on him.

Cabel tried to say something, but I clamped my mouth onto his, rocking forward as he took me in his arms. His hands were firmly planted in my hair when I slammed his back into the mattress. A gasp escaped Cabel's lips as I dug my knees into the bed on either side of his hips.

"But you haven't even opened your present yet," he grunted between kisses.

"Shut up," I growled, hovering over him.

I tasted the smirk on Cabel's lips and pinned his arms above his head, forcing him to submit. He wasn't used to this side of me, and neither was I. But pregnancy had an invisible finger pushing buttons tied directly to my hormones. Just like an enemy sticking pins through a voodoo doll. Only I doubt that felt this good.

I pressed my palm into the pillow beside Cabel's head and slowly descended his body, leaving a trail of kisses from his neck to his chest to his taut, lean stomach. When I reached his mouth again, Cabel sat up in the bed and smoothed my dark tresses along my back. My fingers twirled through the ends of his hair while I teased his lower lip with my teeth.

Cabel groaned and slid his fingers beneath my shirt to make contact with my bare skin, the fabric bunching up around my waist. When he dragged the shirt over the top of my head and cast it aside, I leaned down over him, and my locks brushed against his face.

Enfolding his hands with mine, I touched my lips to Cabel's cheek, and he closed his eyes with the sweetest sigh. In that moment, I studied the image of Cabel with such a relaxed, tranquil expression on his face. He looked like an angel.

* * *

Cabel glanced up at the ceiling and placed his hand over his heart, gasping for air. I tucked my arm around his elbow and kissed his throat. His skin tasted salty, as we were both coated in a sheen of damp sweat.

"Well," he began, still catching his breath. "That was—"

"Different," I finished for him.

He looked into my eyes and turned my chin up in the palm of his hand. "Who are you, and what have you done with my wife?"

A sensual smile peeled across his face, lengthening into a playful smirk. He bit the edge of his lower lip and then traced his thumb nail along mine. I nipped at his thumb, and he didn't withdraw his hand until he felt the outline of my teeth.

"Ow," he reacted, enjoying it. Then he sank his teeth into my lower lip before ending the seductive exchange with a delicate kiss.

We lay there together for the longest time, listening to the elevator chime down the hall mixed with the sound of crushing waves outside. The two of us were cocooned in a blissful state of ecstasy. It was a fragile net of protection that I didn't want to drop.

"Why do you think...?" Cabel left off the end of his sentence, probably too distracted to complete his thought.

I giggled into his chest, prompting him to stare down at me and smile.

"What?" he inquired. "Tell me."

Gnawing on the edge of my lip, I watched him out of the corner of my eye and said, "It's because I'm pregnant."

His icy blue eyes widened, and his lips formed a circular "oh." After nodding in understanding, he looked over me, and there was another smile. "Well, in that case, maybe I should knock you up more often."

Laughter escaped me as Cabel covered my face with kisses. When his hands moved further south, I rubbed my nose against his own. "Can I open my present now?"

Cabel chuckled and held himself above me. "Now there's the woman I married."

Rolling my eyes, I stuck my tongue out at him as he reached for the bag. Once he handed it over, I stuck my hand inside and found a black sweater wrapped in a few sheets of tissue paper. The material was cotton, soft and warm. But when I read the title on the front, my entire being filled with light. The image of a red Santa hat sat atop the words **Mom-To-Be**. While it was the last thing I had expected to receive, that made me all the more grateful to have it.

Without a single word, I slipped my arms through the sleeves and tugged the sweater over my head. **Mom-To-Be** was proudly displayed across my breast, a name that I was more than thrilled to claim. Cabel pulled at my long hair that had been tucked beneath the back of my shirt and let it fall so that the dark strands framed my pale face.

"I know it's not much, but they didn't have that big of a selection in the shop downstairs."

Before he could see the tears welling up in my eyes, I clasped his face in my hands and kissed him with every ounce of energy I had left. Cabel set his fingers on my neck in a gentle caress, then traced his thumb along my cheekbone and pulled back.

"Finley, what's wrong? Why are you crying?"

Through the glistening drops of moisture in my eyes, I gazed at him and smiled. "I'm pregnant."

"Right." He stroked the back of his knuckles against my cheek and then pressed his forehead to mine. "That you are."

Chapter 22

Once Christmas passed, it didn't seem strange to think that we might spend every holiday here. We were together. And for the time being, that was all that mattered.

For some stupid reason, we had gotten brave enough to go out in public without so much as a single disguise. Monty was far away with family for the holidays, yet the media caught wind of his whereabouts every other day. So long as he remained several states in the other direction, we had no cause for concern. Even Cabel insisted that as long as we went out at night, no one would be paying enough attention to catch us.

Believing him merely because I wanted to, I took Cabel's hand every time he offered it. We went out to eat at crowded restaurants, walked along the shore, and even went shopping for clothes at the local boutiques. In the back of my mind, I knew we wouldn't appear anonymous forever. Someone Monty knew might find us, recognize us. But no one ever did. So we kept up with the charade. And that had been our first mistake.

One night, just before the end of the year, Cabel rented a small motor boat and took me out on the water. The moon looked like a great big ball in the sky, watching over us with its pearly luminosity. I kept my eyes on it as we moved farther across the sea, until the hotel had nearly become a speck in the distance.

A cold shiver passed through my parted lips, rattling my teeth to the core. Even though I was dressed and bundled in a warm blanket, the temperature continued to drop every minute we stayed on the water.

By the time I thought to tell Cabel to slow down, that he had gone too far, a beautiful cavern appeared up ahead on the left, jutting out of the rock. I recalled hearing a guest at the hotel talking about sea caves once, as we hurriedly shuffled through the lobby. Cabel decreased our speed and steered the boat into the darkness.

Without the glow of the moonlight, we were at the mercy of whatever lay in these shadowy crevices. Cabel flicked on an oversized flashlight and sat it upright in the boat. My eyes darted to the ceiling that must have been ten stories high. A hushed whimper left me voiceless when I saw black creatures hanging from up above. I looked to Cabel, who didn't seem the least bit affected by the presence of bats overhead.

Trusting my husband, I kept quiet despite the brooding wave of nausea I felt creeping up in my stomach. Before long, we had reached the innermost part of the cave. So Cabel pulled the boat up to where the sea met a bed of flat rock. Then he eyed our surroundings before helping me out.

"What are we doing here, Cabel?" Our recent excursions out into public had been one thing. But bringing me here when neither of us had a clue who or what might be lurking in the dark was pushing it.

"This is where I brought you," Cabel answered. "This is where we came after you fell."

"You mean, after someone pushed me?" I took a step closer and got in his face, unsure why I was so angry all of a sudden. Even now, that night felt like a dream. I still didn't understand everything that had happened.

"Yes." Cabel levelled his eyes at me. "Someone pushed you."

Cabel stuck his hands in his pockets and strode along the rock that bordered the water. Feeling several steps behind, I followed him, keeping at his heels until he turned around to face me.

"What happened that night, Cabel?" I grabbed his arm and pulled. "How did you get me out of the water so fast?"

He looked down at me and swallowed.

"Weren't your hands tied?"

Cabel cocked his head to the side, contemplating what he was willing to share with me and what he wasn't. Like always, Cabel kept more than he revealed.

"Jane cut the rope," he admitted. "They thought if I jumped that there was no way either of us would survive."

I furrowed my brow, and the panic returned to my nervous system ten-fold, comfortably settling in. "That means they know we're still out here. They know we're still alive."

"No. We got away. Trust me. They think we're dead."

"How do you know that? How do you know anything for sure?" My voice carried across the cave, just as I realized I had raised it.

"You would have drowned if I hadn't saved you," he reminded me.

"Saved me from what? We're gonna die anyway!"

The bats overhead flew down and zoomed past us, departing from the cave to explore the open night sky. Fire shot through my system and into my veins, erupting every bit of anger within me. I had been living a lie with a man who thought this was some kind of honeymoon. Monty wanted us dead. When the smoke cleared and he found out that we weren't, then what?

"This is so stupid! I can't believe you thought that we could just stay here!"

If I was furious, then he hadn't seen irate. But to be honest, the one person I was the most mad at was myself.

"Finley, everything will be fine."

"Fine? *Fine?* What part of this is fine?" I flung

my hands in the air and then picked rocks up off the ground and started chucking them at the wall. "I'm. So. Stupid." I threw one stone after the next, yearning for some type of release from the anger I felt, the anxiety, the fear. Always the fear.

"Finley, stop." Cabel reached out for me, but I fought against him, still too upset to allow any room for comfort. He grasped my elbows in his hands and then forced my arms at my sides. I was still so angry, thrashing and cursing about, until he imprisoned me with his arms locked around my torso. "Stop," he cooed, his breath raining down my neck.

And that was when I started to cry.

The tears came in heart-startling sobs, all-consuming and bone-chilling. They would find us. They would kill us. And I would never get to meet my baby girl. Cayley would remain a pipe dream, just like the false reality that we could have a long, happy life together. That was never destined for us in a world where Monty and Jane exist.

"I have a plan," Cabel revealed. "I've had a plan all along. You're just going to have to trust me." He waited a beat before adding, "Do you trust me?"

I nodded my head, and he turned me around to face him.

"I'm not gonna let anything happen to you." He cradled my face in his hands, and then moved one of his palms to my belly. "I'm not gonna let anything happen to our little girl."

I quivered before him and looked deep into his eyes. They hardly looked blue in the dark. But there was something so familiar about them, while at the same time appearing distant. Even now, I knew there were things Cabel was keeping from me. But that's just how he was. One day, I was going to have to accept the fact that I had married a man who kept secrets from me. But maybe some secrets were better left alone.

The feel of Cabel's hand on my stomach sent a pulsing warmth through my body. Once I parted my lips out of instinct, Cabel brought his mouth to mine, and I shuddered. He tore his fingers through my hair and slammed my body into his, warming my cold lips, my cold skin.

Cabel picked me up in his arms, his palms searing through the back of my thighs. When he pressed me up against the wall of the cave, I could hardly breathe. He consumed my mouth, tugging and coaxing, and I couldn't bear another second apart. While I didn't know it that night, it would be one of the last times he loved me for a while.

Chapter 23

O nce we returned to the hotel, I longed for a hot bath and wanted nothing more than for Cabel to climb in there with me. As I caught myself daydreaming in the elevator, Cabel pulled me into his side and squeezed tight. He knew how to touch me in a way that would make me believe anything he said. But it wasn't until we made it back to the room that reality twisted around my heart with the claw-like force of the Grim Reaper, and the bubble burst.

The moment I stepped across the threshold, something seemed off. For starters, the entire suite looked pristine, like someone had scrubbed the floors and dusted the furniture until every available surface sparkled. I didn't tell Cabel anything, waiting for him to mention the noticeable change on his own.

Continuing through the suite, I stepped into the bedroom to find quarters that barely looked lived in. The bed was made, every pillow stacked in perfect assembly. The covers were even turned down, as if someone had expected our arrival before bed time.

As my heart throbbed loudly inside my chest, the thrumming in my ears attune to the same rhythm, Cabel stripped his clothes off and hopped in the shower. Typical man. Never pay attention to the details until they've slapped you in the face. I could have scolded him for not noticing the change. But maybe the difference was so slight that he would think I was crazy. He would think I was making it up. Or worse, that I was absolutely paranoid.

Trying to keep my cool, I opened the closet and found all of our clothes hung in a nice, neat, color-coded fashion. While we both were keen on organization, I had never gone to the extent of assembling a rainbow of outfits as my wardrobe. Observing the rearranged clothes, I caught a whiff of something sweet in the air. In that moment, it occurred to me that I had recognized the odor as soon as we entered our room. Once I walked into the bathroom and shut the door behind me, the enclosing kept the heat in, as well as the smell. Just like that, my instincts proved worthy, and I was right.

Jane had been here, because the entire suite reeked with the scent of cotton candy.

"Cabel?"

"Yeah," he answered from the shower.

"Did you notice anything different about our hotel room?"

"Right now?"

"When you walked in the door."

He hesitated for a moment, then said, "No. Why?"

I opened the glass door and stepped inside. "Someone's been here."

Cabel turned around and rinsed the shampoo out of his hair. When he wouldn't respond, I understood immediately. No matter what I said, he would write every observation off as the direct result of paranoia.

"The floors have been scrubbed. The bed is made. And all of our clothes are hanging in the closet like some sort of color coordinated rainbow!"

The rise and fall of my chest couldn't be helping, but I knew what I was talking about. I had seen it all with my own eyes. And if he wouldn't just look around and notice it too, then it was because he was in denial.

"Finley, calm down," he said, his blue eyes especially light and husky. "It's probably just the maid service."

"Really?" I set my hands on my hips and glowered. "Then why is the Do Not Disturb sign still hanging on the door?"

"Maybe they didn't see it," he suggested.

"It's Jane!" I projected my voice, making it very clear to Cabel that he was going to hear me whether he wanted to or not. "She was here."

Cabel stilled beneath the shower, eyeing me carefully from where he was standing. "What makes you say that?"

Combing my fingers through my hair, I closed my eyes and scowled. Why couldn't he just believe me?

"Her perfume," I claimed.

"What?"

"Her perfume! The whole place smells like cotton candy!"

Cabel watched me out of the corner of his eye and then said, "I didn't notice."

"Ugh! Well would you at least admit that someone was here?"

Cabel grabbed a bar of soap and began lathering his arms. And while his biceps flexed in a way that made my insides turn to mush, I wasn't done proving my point.

"Yes. It was the maid service. I already told you that."

Gritting my teeth, I stepped out of the shower and slammed the door behind me. I wasn't crazy. Jane had been here, which surely meant she would be back.

That night I could hardly sleep, still boiling over with anger. I tossed and turned until the sheets were all twisted and tangled. Cabel slept soundly beside me, as if he'd never had a care in the world. Even though it should have been his concern, for the rest of the night I slept with one eye open.

Chapter 24

On New Year's Eve, I stood in front of the bathroom mirror, hardly able to believe my appearance. I was wearing a formal ball gown of black satin and lace. The skirting nearly swept the floor, though I was thankful for the elevated stature provided by my high heels, as they were surprisingly easy to maneuver in.

Cabel dressed in a suit and tie, his blonde hair combed back in a presentable manner. When he watched me enter the bedroom, still adjusting his tie, I would be lying if I said that I didn't enjoy the look of desire in his crystal blue eyes. But I was still too angry, feeling as though I had been dealt an unfair hand and everyone could see my cards. After Jane's ghost-like presence in our room, I knew danger was near, lurking and looming before us. What I couldn't fathom was why Cabel couldn't see it.

"You look beautiful."

I glowered at Cabel and moved towards him, crossing my arms over my chest. He placed his hand on my back and steered me in front of the mirror, as we both eyed my reflection. The strapless gown was lovely, exposing my bare shoulders and the piece of ribbon around my neck. My russet tresses hung down in soft, natural waves, since I had just washed my hair in the shower.

We looked fit for a ball, but all I wanted was to go home. To a place where the illusion of a daydream didn't feel like such a nightmare.

"This is stupid," I griped. "We shouldn't be here. We should have left and gone somewhere else days ago. Why would you bring me here?"

Cabel gnawed at the edge of his lip and leaned back against the dresser, his eyes cast down. I knew that my attitude had been nothing but sour as of late. And yet, I couldn't stop myself. Nothing felt right or safe or real anymore. I was tired of playing this charade. Surely, Monty had been given plenty of time to discover us by now. Didn't Cabel care about our safety? Didn't he care about our little girl?

"I promise this is our last night."

"Of what?" I cocked my eyebrow at him, misunderstanding.

"We'll check out in the morning," he explained. "It will be a new year. We'll start off fresh."

"And go where?"

"Can't you just trust me to take care of you? To take care of us?"

"Oh, like you've done so far?" I turned on my heel and sat down on the edge of the mattress.

What bothered me most was that there was something he was not telling me. It was eating away at my core and pushing the love I felt for him aside.

Cabel sighed and reached into his pocket. "Here," he said, offering me the extra room key. "Since you're already sick of me tonight."

I took the plastic card from him and stared at the name of the hotel written on the front. So we were destined to spend the night alone. My first New Year's that I wasn't single, and now I wouldn't even have someone to kiss when the clock struck twelve.

"Can't you at least see things from my perspective? For once?"

Cabel moved towards me and breathed down my neck. "Can't you see them from mine?"

While I stood there sulking, he opened the closet and leaned inside. Apparently, the hotel hosted an annual New Year's Eve party in one of the large ballrooms downstairs. There would be food, drinks, live entertainment, and dancing, followed by the ritualistic spectacle of fireworks out on the beach. I was neither hungry nor thirsty, and I sure didn't feel like dancing. But Cabel had convinced me that we needed a night out, that we had been cooped up together too long, that no one here knew who we were anyway.

"Turn around," Cabel commanded.

I did as he said, and he set a black mask over the top of my face, though it mainly covered my temples, as well as the skin above and beneath my eyes. He tied the thick ribbon attached to the mask at the back of my head and then covered the knot with a pile of my hair. When I glanced into the mirror, I studied the intricate detailings that had been painted onto the mask. Silver stars and flowers. White lines and swirls. The image was startling, because the designs on the mask were distracting, even to those who might find me recognizable.

Cabel slipped a mask on that covered his entire face, except for open circles that had been cut out for his eyes. A dark band fit around the back of his head, slipping between his blonde tresses. When he looked in the glass, I gasped at the frozen, two-faced expression of the mask he wore. The left side of his face was solid white, while the right side was nothing but black, his blue eyes the only indication that I was still standing by my husband.

He looked like a joker with a split face, except the mouth on his mask remained positively straight. Neither a smile nor a frown. Just a totally inhuman expression.

"Remember what I told you," he declared, though the fact that I could no longer see his mouth move left me a little scared. The mask was not a cheerful one, and I felt a chill creep up my spine when he looked into my eyes. "Finley."

"Yes, I remember."

"If anything happens, go to the cave where I

took you the other night. I'll meet you there." The words vibrated against the mask over his face, and when he grabbed my arms, I flinched. "Finley, it's just me."

"I know." I looked down and then brought my eyes up to meet his. "You just look kind of creepy in that thing is all."

"It's just a mask." He patted my shoulder and then squeezed my hand, rubbing his thumb over my wedding ring.

Following suit, I grabbed his wrist and ran my fingertips over his golden wedding band and beneath the knuckle where I had placed it. Despite everything that had happened, I did love him, no matter who he was. Perhaps he had kept more secrets from me than I would ever care to know. But that's what had always drawn me to Cabel Jones, my perfect golden boy. The mystery.

"Are you expecting something to?"

"What?" Cabel touched my arm and then lifted my chin in his hand.

"Earlier." I held his frosty blue gaze. "When you said if anything happens. Are you expecting something to happen tonight?"

Cabel replied without blinking. "No."

"You're lying," I noted.

"Look, nothing's gonna happen, all right? Just believe me."

My eyes dropped to the floor and I nodded. He was lying, but so was I. Though he may have been lying to keep my stress level low for the sake of the baby, I didn't see how hiding the truth had ever been a way to protect me. But it was in Cabel's nature to conceal matters from me that he believed were better left unsaid for my own good. The deeper I sank into ignorance, the more I began to question whether or not I really knew my husband at all.

"Nobody is going to recognize us, Finley. Besides, they'll all be wearing masks."

I nodded my head again and gazed into his eyes. Surely, we couldn't be more safe than in a sea of strangers. But as I stared into those clear pools of cool, glowing light, I saw fear, doubt, and worry.

Knowing that I very well may be walking into a trap and taking Cabel with me, I lifted the mask off his face and stroked the stubble of his beard one last time. Our eyes met, and he saw the sadness in mine. Cabel leaned down and delicately brushed his fingers along my jaw as I shut my eyes. Then he pulled me in and crushed his lips to mine, sending a wave of electricity beneath the surface of my skin. I folded my arms around him and forced him into my body with my hand clinging to the back of his neck.

Cabel gasped and returned his mouth to mine, his hands grabbing and squeezing at my sides. He moaned as a soft whimper shook my voice, my fingernails digging into the ends of his hair. When he pushed forward and set me down on the mattress, it wasn't long before the fabric of my dress was riding up to my thighs. We lay down together, and Cabel made me sigh.

I think we both knew the end was near.

Chapter 25

O nce we reached the lobby, Cabel and I took the stairs that led to the grand ballroom. There was a gloriously expensive glass chandelier that hung overhead, momentarily hypnotizing and distracting me. Cabel rested his hand at the small of my back and led me into the swarm of strangers, who were even more so beneath the veil of masked disguise.

There were women in evening gowns that looked like something out of a cook book full of pastries. Peachy silks. Lime linens. Aqua satins. Magenta jewels. All of the men wore tuxes and matching masks of the black and white variety. While the patterns were all distinct designs, some solid colored, some checkered, some striped, the masks that looked closest to Cabel's were nearly identical. To avoid losing him, I would have to stay close by his side for the remainder of the night.

When I spotted the lush buffet that lined the left side of the room, my eyes widened with hunger. Seeing the expression on my face, Cabel led me towards the abundant supply of food and handed me a plate. Although we had already eaten dinner, I helped myself to a piece of steak and pasta salad. Since I was pregnant, there was always room for dessert, so I selected a small bowl of orange sorbet to cool my temperature and chill my nerves.

"Better?" Cabel asked, sitting quietly beside me. He drummed his fingers over a stack of napkins at our nearly empty table. But I was thankful for the share of the room that we had to ourselves.

"Yep." I dabbed each corner of my mouth with a cloth napkin and tossed it over my empty plate.

When the band began to play a slow tune, Cabel nudged my shoulder, and I wished I could have seen through that thick mask, because I swear he was smiling. As irony would have it, the next song on the set list was "Me & Mrs. Jones," an old R & B ballad that in some ways felt like the story of my life. Cabel took my hand and dragged me onto the dance floor, where we found a spot among the crowd of masked strangers.

Cabel let one hand slide to the small of my back, while the other gently clasped my palm. We softly swayed back and forth, until I put my head on his chest, sleepy from the food and music. In that moment, the people around us seemed to disappear, and when I look back now, that was the last moment I had with the Cabel I knew. But it was a tender moment regardless, and I wished that

I could have seen what was coming as we shared it.

Once the music stopped, I leaned forward to whisper in Cabel's ear. He nodded as everyone applauded the band, and I scurried from the ballroom unseen.

In the lobby, I found the nearest restroom and relieved myself of the three glasses of punch I had consumed with my second dinner. Exiting the stall, I caught sight of my strange appearance as I walked towards the ever-widening mirror above an army of sinks. I almost laughed at the ridiculous nature of my entire ensemble. The dress and the mask and the hair. But maybe Cabel had wanted our last night here to be light-hearted. My mind briefly flashed back to his talk of going on the honeymoon we never had. Was that what all of this had been about? Some bucket list for newlyweds? The thought unsettled me, because who would make a bucket list if you weren't about to kick it?

Suddenly, a glimpse of red made my heart flutter, and I wondered if I had just seen a ghost. Drying my hands with a paper towel, I tossed it in the garbage and rushed outside. In the lobby, I saw no sign of red anywhere, though there was a very clear image in my head of a woman in a crimson dress. Once I spotted Cabel, I sighed with relief and rushed after him into the ballroom.

But when I reached the man in the black and white mask, he was clinging to a woman in a lavender gown, her own mask decorated with plume feathers the color of fuchsia. Feeling confused, I turned back to the table where we had been sitting earlier, but he was gone. Heat rose beneath my skin, making me feel hot all over. Nausea was brewing deep in the pit of my stomach, as I stumbled across the dance floor in search of my husband. Though I had been calling his name, the music was far too loud for even my own ears to hear.

Just when it seemed that all was lost, I noticed a man with golden blonde hair that reflected the light. Though his back was to me, I had an instinctual feeling that I had found him at last. Storming through the crowd, I reached the man and tugged on his shoulder until he spun around to face me. The mask he wore was split down the middle, all black on the right, all white on the left, and he even had a gold wedding band on.

But then I looked into his eyes, and my heart became lodged in my chest. Or perhaps I had swallowed it, because I hardly seemed able to breathe. While every other indicator pointed to the fact that he was my husband, I did not have the fortune of admiring his light blue eyes as they stared back at me. Though it pained me to admit it, I had found the wrong guy. This man's eyes were green.

Fear rippled through me as I rushed out of the ballroom and up the staircase, through the lobby and into the first available elevator. My finger stabbed the button to the floor of our hotel room faster than anyone could join me on the ride up. I gripped the cool metal of the handrail and forced the bile down my throat. By the time the elevator reached the correct floor, I raced to the room and opened the door with my key card. I flung my mask onto the kitchen counter and heard the door click shut behind me, then headed straight into the bedroom and the bathroom attached. In an instant, I was down on my knees in front of the toilet and puking up everything I had eaten in the past hour.

Once that horrid moment passed, I flushed the toilet and leaned my head back against the wall. Even though my face was covered in clammy moisture, I felt goosebumps breaking out all along the surface of my skin. While I wanted to write off my sudden sickness as pregnancy related, I couldn't be sure if it had been caused by the food or not.

Rising to my feet, I nearly collapsed on my way to the sink, where I eventually garnered the strength to rinse my mouth out with water and then brush my teeth. I needed to reapply some makeup and fix my hair before I went downstairs and continued my search for Cabel. He obviously wasn't here, and I had no desire to be alone on a night like this, when my husband was nowhere in sight.

With my head down, I shuffled into the bedroom and leaned against the wall. Nearly closing my eyes, I brushed my fingers through my hair on my journey to the kitchen. A glass of tap water. That was all I would need to regain my bearings and go find my husband.

As I leaned against the kitchen counter and drained the glass, I noticed something sitting in the empty fruit basket by the fridge. Or at least the fruit basket that had been empty when I left with Cabel for the evening. Setting my glass aside, I crept closer to the basket and a single green apple was resting at the center of it.

My blood turned cold, but I reached my hand out and claimed the fruit, reminiscent of the poison apple from *Snow White*. Not wanting to believe that something so perfectly staged could be real, I thickly swallowed and turned the fruit over in the palm of my hand. A bright red kiss stood out against the light green color of the peel, and I gasped in terror, dropping the apple as it rolled across the floor.

Trying to be smart for the sake of my baby, I quietly stepped out of my shoes and then inched my way towards the living room. As I searched for more signs of an intruder, my eyes connected with the mirror on the wall, and I stepped closer with the speed of a wary doe.

Smeared on the glass in red lipstick were the words *Mrs. Jones.* My name was surrounded by a large heart with thick curves and jagged edges. Just as I felt the world spinning beneath my feet, Jane appeared in the mirror behind my reflection, and I screamed.

Chapter 26

Once the terror left my lungs, I braced myself for whatever Jane had planned. Before I could turn around, she was already coming towards me, and I knew the crimson dress she wore was the flash of red I had glimpsed earlier. I ran from her, circling the dining room table, though she remained at my heels.

When she got close enough to pull my hair, I spun around and slapped her. She stumbled back and gritted her teeth, so I jerked a chair out from the table and tossed it at her. Since she ducked before the chair could do any actual damage, I tipped the table over and hoped that it would pin her beneath it.

Assuming that she would find a way to continue chasing me anyway, I slid over the kitchen counter and opened the utensil drawer to retrieve a knife. Once I had the weapon firmly gripped in my hand, Jane froze in front of the toppled over table and chairs. Whether she knew it or not, Jane had messed with the wrong pregnant lady.

"Don't come any closer!" I warned, aiming the

sharp blade at her. Jane took a step back and eyed me warily, perhaps underestimating what I was willing to do to survive.

"I'm not here to hurt you, Finley. I just want to talk."

"Really?" I hissed. "About what?"

"Your husband," she countered.

"What about him?" I said through a pair of gritted teeth.

"We're going to be together," she insisted. "He doesn't love you. He loves me. And he's going to leave you for me."

"Cabel would never leave me," I claimed.

Jane moved farther away from me and sat down on the coffee table in front of the couch. She examined her cuticle beds and didn't seem the least bit frightened at all. "Really? Why not?"

"Because I'm pregnant with his child!" I shouted, feeling the veins throb in my neck.

"Monty said that was a lie to keep Cabel from divorcing you," she scoffed. "You're not pregnant."

"Yes I am!"

"Well then." Jane slid off the edge of the coffee table and walked around the couch, slithering towards me. "Why don't we find out?"

I heard the clicking sound of a door opening, and Cabel slipped inside. As soon as the door shut, he rushed over to me and snatched the knife out of my hand. I wondered what had happened to his mask.

"What are you doing?" He put the knife in the drawer and jerked my arm, digging his fingernails into my flesh until it hurt.

"Ow! Let go of me!" I squirmed within Cabel's hold, but he dragged me into the living room until I plopped down on the couch in front of Jane.

"Tell her, Cabel," she commanded. "There's no point in making the poor girl suffer anymore."

Losing my grip on the couch cushion, I glanced up at Cabel with confusion and fear in my eyes.

"Fine then," Jane barked. "I'll tell her."

She picked up the remote control and turned the TV on, flipping through channels until she reached a news station. My jaw dropped once my eyes settled on the headline racing across the screen. It couldn't be true. It just couldn't.

Presidential Hopeful Found Dead In Home

The announcer rattled off some nonsense about Monty having a heart attack after dinner the previous night. I glanced up at the apathetic expression on Jane's face and knew she had been involved. Her connection to Monty had never been public knowledge, and I had no evidence proving that she had instigated the death of her father. And yet, I knew what she had done.

"Why did you do it?"

Jane turned the TV off, and the subtle blue glow that had been bouncing off her face disappeared. I looked over at Cabel, but he had become a different person, his eyes sinking to the floor. Shouldn't he have been concerned? Shouldn't he have been scared?

"He never loved me," she confessed. "I didn't even know who he was until four years ago." She tossed the remote across the coffee table, as I heard it scratch the glass. "I wasn't about to let him take the only thing I care about away from me."

I opened my mouth to speak, but then she said something more.

"He deserved it."

Furrowing my brow, I watched the expression of indifference on my husband's face and shuddered. Wasn't he going to do something? Say something? Have any sort of reaction at all?

"Well," Jane began, standing before us with both her hands on her hips. "Aren't you going to tell her, Cabey?"

CABEY?

Fire shot out of my eyes and then rippled beneath the surface of my skin. When she approached Cabel and wrapped her arms around him, he didn't move. He didn't welcome her touch, but he made no attempt to fight her off either.

"Jane and I are getting married," he dully announced. "I'll give you the divorce like you asked for, Finley. You can take whatever you want."

Feeling as though I had just had the wind knocked out of me, I stared into Cabel's eyes and sat there for an entire minute just gaping at the two of them. This could not be happening. I must have been stuck in some kind of bad dream.

"Aren't you glad I kept the ring?" Jane wore a white diamond on her third finger, and I was ready to vomit all over again. "All those years ago, but I never forgot you, Cabey."

Rising to my feet, I glanced at them both in horror. "So it's true then? You have been having an affair!"

"Yes," Jane answered.

"I'm talking to my husband," I growled back.

"Soon to be ex-husband," she snipped.

Though I was overcome with shock and outrage, I felt like a complete idiot. Monty may have planned to terminate us both, in case we ever revealed his dealings with Blain Ulrich in the forest. But Jane had arrived with her own agenda and foiled her father's plans beautifully. Of course Cabel had insisted that we stay here. That had given Jane plenty of time to eliminate Monty.

She had cut the rope on Cabel's wrists and let him jump into the ocean after me, because she was counting on him to live. But now that Monty posed no threat to Cabel's life, what was she planning to do with me?

"He was mine first," Jane proclaimed, interrupting my thoughts. "And he'll be mine last."

I studied Cabel's posture and mannerisms carefully, while Jane went on and on about how happy the two of them were going to be together. But then I saw it, that unblinking gaze of solemn

surrender in Cabel's crystal blue eyes.
   He was lying.

Chapter 27

C abel," I called, angling my face towards him. "Tell me this isn't true. Tell me that you're both lying."

He hung his head in shame, and I watched her skinny fingers coil around his neck. Jane grinned at me out of enjoyment for the sheer fact that she had won. But Cabel wasn't some trophy, some object to be trifled with and fought over. Jane wanted to own him. All I had ever needed was his love.

"Cabel, at least tell her that I'm pregnant." I touched his shoulder until he looked into my eyes. "Own up to it."

Jane scoffed, brushing the matter off. "You're not pregnant. I don't know the first man that would lay his hands on you."

Rolling my eyes at the hurtful insult of her remark, I held Cabel's gaze and he relented. The baby was in my body, under my protection, in my womb. For that matter, I didn't fear her safety. But my heart had yet to shatter again, because I didn't believe anything Jane had to say. It was Cabel's word that I was calling into question. How much of the past month had been the truth? And how much had been a lie?

"Finley's pregnant," Cabel announced. "It's not a lie."

Jane gasped in astonishment, and I'd be lying if I said that I didn't enjoy the satisfaction. But then Cabel cut deeper than the knife he had taken out of my hand. And I knew that no one knew that man, my husband, better than me.

"I don't love, Jane. I've never loved you. And you don't love me either. You don't know me."

"Cabel," she whined, rubbing his arm. "Of course I know you. What about that night we spent together in Paris?"

"I've never been to Paris."

"Cabey, what are you talking about?"

"I've never even been out of the country."

She ruffled her fingers through her hair in confusion. "Yes, you have," she insisted. "That summer we spent together in Europe. Come on," she nudged, growing scared and angry. "We got matching tattoos. Don't you remember?"

The expression on Cabel's face turned stoic. "I've never gotten a tattoo. I hate needles."

Jane turned her back on him and cried, "What are you talking about?"

I had seen Cabel without a stitch of clothing on more times than not, and there wasn't a drop of ink on his naked body. Jane must have been more out of her mind than I thought. Maybe she was just delusional. Or crazy.

With her back to us, Jane lifted the skirt of her dress as Cabel stepped back to stand beside me. I leaned into his side, holding on tight when she spun towards us with rage. There was a black tattoo etched in a scripted font over her left hip, as well as an image of the Eiffel tower beside it. When she glared at Cabel, demanding that he do the same, I lingered behind him and crossed my arms over my chest.

Without showing the least bit of emotion, Cabel untucked his shirt and unbuckled his pants, revealing either of his bare, tattoo-less hips to us both. While the sight held no significance to me—I already knew Cabel had never covered his body with ink—Jane collapsed to the floor. My eyes widened at the sight of her, as I considered the distance to the nearest psych ward.

"No!" she wailed, covering her mouth. A series of loud, strangled sobs escaped her shivering lips, and I couldn't understand what was wrong with her. "He's gone," she cried. "Cabel's gone."

While she wept uncontrollably on the floor, I turned to my husband with wide-set eyes. My blood was running cold, and I could feel a dull, aching throb beginning to form in my chest. Pain lingered in my stomach—a sense of nausea that wasn't pregnancy related.

"Cabel, what is she talking about?" For the first time, when I looked at my husband, all I felt was fear. I moved around the couch and took several steps towards the overturned table and chairs, slowly backing away from him.

"Finley, it's me," he declared, walking closer.

"Who are you?" I whispered as tears felt like stinging pin pricks in my eyes.

"Baby, please." He reached out for me, and I stumbled over one of the chairs.

"He's lying!" Jane hollered across the floor. "He's been lying this whole time!"

I cocked my head up at Cabel, my whole body quivering. "What is she talking about?"

He knelt down before me and held my face in his hands. "I'm not who you think I am."

My body tensed in reaction to his touch. Though the gentle caress was familiar, I no longer knew who I could trust. Some underlying instinct buried deep within my soul compelled me to look into his eyes and say, "What's your real name?"

Cabel stared down at the ground, and his hands dropped from my face. When he answered me, it was with a small, yet pained whisper. "Seth."

Just like that, the whole word spun out from under me, and I knew that I was going to be sick. Perhaps Jane wasn't actually crazy. Maybe I was the one who had lost her mind.

The truth hit me like a ton of bricks. Why everything had been so strange. Why nothing seemed to make sense. Why my life and marriage and resolve had all felt like they were slipping away.

Cabel had died years ago in my arms. And I had unknowingly married his twin brother instead.

But what hurt the most was the fact that I had not only fallen for it. I had let him touch a part of me that no other ever had. While I had thought this baby was the product of my love for Cabel, nothing that I had once believed was true anymore.

I was carrying the child of another man.

Chapter 28

No," I cried, soft tears streaming down from my eyes. Of all the lies I had been told, why did this one have to be true? "No."

He grabbed my arms to hold me tight, and I didn't know what to call him. He still looked like Cabel to me.

"Shh, Finley, it's still me. I swear." He pressed his forehead against mine, and I quivered at the way his familiar breath danced over my neck. "Please. Believe me."

And there were those words again. The words of my husband, the father of my child begging me to have faith in his word, even when reason proved against it. But I did not know this man, this liar, this deceptive doppelganger. The way he touched me now made my skin run icy cold, despite the fact that I was sweating bullets.

I felt like vomiting.

I felt like fleeing.

I felt like my whole life had become some sad dream that I no longer wished to be a part of.

"Finley." His hands were on my face, touching and caressing and soothing.

But I didn't want to be soothed.

"No!" I ripped his hands away from me and took several steps back.

"Baby, it's still me," he pleaded.

"No, it's not!" I shouted, searching his crystal blue eyes. Of course they would look the same. Of course they would be the same. But they were not.

"We can't trust him, Finley," Jane advised, picking herself up off the floor.

Fisting my hands in my hair, I walked into the bedroom and crumpled to the ground. I was so confused. There was no right and wrong anymore. No good and evil. No truth and lie. It was all the same, converging and digressing into a series of blurred lines. And I had been fool enough to dance between them.

Several knocks on the door sent me reeling.

"Hotel security," a firm voice announced.

"I'll handle this," Jane volunteered, rearranging herself in the mirror before she nodded to open the door.

My husband, stranger that he now was, came into the bedroom and shut the door behind us. When our eyes met, mine had pooled over with so many tears that I could hardly see. He reached out and grabbed me, holding my body securely within his frame.

"I know how all of this sounds, and if you'll just let me explain—"

I pulled away from him and walked over to the window, staring out at the shimmering ocean beneath the moonlight. Fireworks burst into the night sky, dancing and scattering across a tapestry of black. With every flash of light, I looked farther and farther out across the sea, until I could make out the edge of that cavern in the distance. The cave that Cabel had said to retreat to if anything happened. But I didn't know who that Cabel was anymore. The man standing behind me. The man who had placed this child inside of me. My hand moved to my stomach out of instinct, and I feared for my little girl's life more than I had ever feared for my own.

"I love you," he said, dropping to his knees before me. His hands cupped either side of my belly, and I tensed. "And I love that baby." He kissed the fabric over my abdomen. "Our baby."

I didn't know what to believe. My mind flashed back over all the time we had spent together. And while I couldn't believe that I had let him touch me like that, the truth remained. The baby growing inside of me was his.

The door to the bedroom creaked open, and Jane stepped inside. "They're gone."

I regarded her from where I stood by the window, while my husband remained on his knees before me, clinging to my stomach, perhaps reaching for the life beneath it. His gaze remained on me, but I saw fire blaze across Jane's blue eyes. Just like that, she charged for us both, and my husband rose up to protect me. To protect us.

But Jane was too quick for him, as she cracked

a flower vase over his head that I had recalled seeing on the coffee table in the living room. His body slumped to the floor, and he was out cold. In that moment, I realized that Jane wasn't staring at me. Her eyes were readily fixed on my stomach.

"Jane," I gasped, backing into the window. My hands were shaking because she had just sent hotel security away. My only defense.

"You can't have it all!" she screamed. "You can't have my life!"

"Jane, what are you talking about?" I croaked. Then my eyes widened at the sight of the blade in her hand. It was the knife I had held earlier. The knife Cabel had taken away from me. The knife he had placed back in the silverware drawer.

"NOOOO!" I shrieked, hopping up onto the bed and running across it to reach the bathroom.

Before I could make it, Jane snatched my elbow back and tossed me across the floor. Though my ears were ringing, I forced myself onto my feet and punched her in the mouth when she came at me again. Her head snapped back at the contact, and the knife slipped out of her hand.

As I stretched my fingers out to grab the handle before it toppled to the floor, Jane pulled my hair and I screamed. Somehow, my husband managed to startle awake on the floor. But Jane dragged me to the bathroom and locked me inside.

My head banged against the edge of the counter as I crumpled to the tile floor. Deep down, I knew Jane was evil and sadistic. But more relevant than that, I knew what had set her off. The sight of Cabel's identical twin taking pride and joy in the existence of our baby had been too much for her. She was a woman scorned. And being the only woman in the bathroom that the man standing outside of it wanted, I would have to be punished for it.

"What are you going to do? Kill me?" I challenged. "Cabel's gone! Cabel's dead! And when they find out what you did to Monty, you'll be as good as—"

She knocked me in the jaw, and I was seeing stars before my head hit the floor again. When there was blood in my teeth and tears in my dress, Jane set the knife down and glared at me. I saw nothing but vengeance in her eyes.

"I don't want to kill you," Jane proclaimed.

"Finley!" He banged outside on the door, reminding me of our fights as a couple, when I would retreat to the bathroom and lock him out.

"I just want to make you suffer." Jane stood over me and lifted her foot in the air, dressed in a spike-heeled shoe.

"NOOOO!" I cried because I knew where this was headed.

"FINLEY!" He called, slamming into the door, though he had yet to break it.

Without another word, Jane kicked me with as much force as possible right in the stomach. I doubled over, gasping for air, because she had knocked the wind and every good part of life right out of me. When I wrapped my arms around my belly to protect the baby, she sliced the backs of my hands until they moved. Then she kicked me in the stomach again and again, always exuding just as must force, if not more.

Black spots danced over my eyes when my husband busted the door down, and the sheer force slammed into Jane, knocking her unconscious. He leaned down over me and lifted my head in his hands. "Finley," he cried, though I could hardly hear or see.

In the end, it was too late.

It was much too late.

Part III

The New Friend

Chapter 29

Blood and pain. That was all I felt, all I could touch and taste and see. The pulse thrumming in my ears was so strong that I would have rather vomited to rid myself of the pounding rhythm. But the crimson was merely an outfit, a wardrobe, a disguise designed to mask the pain. Hot writhing agony was all-consuming, as I learned the moment I woke up in that hospital bed.

"Finley, Finley," a grating voice declared. "Calm down. You need to breathe."

Blinded by tears, I glared up at the nurse as her fingernails cut into my wrists. Sweat was pouring down my back and dripping down the sides of my neck. And all the while there was nothing but pain.

Pain on the surface. Pain from within. Even pain that I seemed to be experiencing outside of my body. Torture. Agony. Affliction.

It was all the same, because it was all pain.

"Ma'am?" The nurse shook my shoulders frantically, and all I wanted to do was scream. "Calm down, Finley!"

I lolled my head back against the elevated part

of the bed, as she wiped my face with a cool washcloth.

"Finley, I need you to talk to me."

I felt dizzy and light-headed, like no one had even given me the chance to breathe.

"Finley, is that your husband?"

Following the direction her finger pointed, I spotted a window directly across the room and found Seth standing on the other side of it. At that moment, I realized that Cabel had never been my husband at all, that I had married a stranger, that the man I loved had disappeared a long time ago. My life was a sham.

"Finley!" he yelled, banging his fist so hard that it rattled the glass.

"Yes," I rasped, quietly watching him beat against the window.

The nurse left my side and headed for the door.

"No," I begged, a subtle panic fluttering through me. "Don't let him in."

She wore a look of confusion on her face, but made a quick phone call afterwards anyway. Soon, I saw a pair of orderlies take him away, though he fought and swore the whole time. Even as he disappeared from my sight, I remembered thinking how good he had always looked in a suit and tie, since he was still wearing one from the masquerade bash earlier that night.

Not much remained clear to me after that. I was hardly conscious enough to know where or who I was. Flickering lights and beeping machines kept me awake for seconds at a time. But then there was nothing more than blackness all over again. If only it had felt better than the red.

When I finally came to, all I can recall was sunlight shining through the blinds over the window. Although my body ached, what I mostly felt was numb. There was no life left in me. All I wanted to do was scream.

Forcing my eyes open, I noticed Seth sitting in a chair propped up against the wall across from me. He looked like he hadn't slept all night, but my husband perked up at the first sign that I was awake. If only I could have appeared as eager.

"Hey," Seth whispered, still wearing his white dress shirt and black slacks from the night before.

I didn't want to speak to him, because I didn't want to speak to anybody. But the ice cold gleam in his brilliant blue eyes was just so startling, so breathtaking, that I knew he must have been more than a stranger to me. Deep down, there had to be some shred of Cabel left inside of him.

"How are you feeling?" He sat down on the edge of the cot, searching my face. I could see the pain and sorrow all over his.

Holding his gaze, I took a deep breath and confessed, "I lost the baby."

Seth nodded as tears began to glisten in his eyes. When he reached for my hand, I jerked it away, preventing him from making physical contact. The hurt I caused him flashed across his features, but I didn't regret it immediately. It was hard to because I was drowning in my own tortured affliction.

After turning away from me, Seth rose from the bed and leaned against the wall. I heard him crying and knew that I should have offered him comfort, that I should have felt the same, that I should have clung to him with everything I had. But I just couldn't.

"Get out," I growled, my voice turning low.

Seth glanced over at me, appalled that I could be so cruel, apathetic, and heartless. But he had been all of those things and left me childless as a result. His tendency to keep secrets from me had snowballed into a pack of lies that I could neither forgive nor forget.

He had hurt me in more ways than he knew how. And I had failed at protecting my helpless baby, my little girl. She'd never even have a chance. And I didn't even know who her father was.

"How can you be so cold?" Seth dried his eyes with his shirtsleeves, and I listened to the sound of his shoes treading over the floor. Just when I thought he was nearly gone, Seth turned around. "You're not the only one who lost her, you know." He pressed his lips together and shuddered. "She was my child, too."

He opened the door, and it slammed shut behind him so fast that I flinched. Suddenly, burning hot tears filled my eyes, as my hand landed over my belly out of habit. For weeks, I had been dreaming of this baby. My little girl. Cabel's little girl. Our little girl.

Pain ripped through me while I buried my head in the pillow and mourned her death in silence. My entire body shook with the force of each agonizing sob. I cried out in agony and sank my teeth into my lower lip with such force that it began to bleed.

The truth was that all of my hopes and dreams had been tied up in that baby. She had been the glue that would bind us together. She was a flicker of hope to a pair of orphans, who would finally be able to start a family of their own. But now she was gone, and I didn't even have Cabel's shoulder to cry on.

When I began making too much noise, the nurse rushed in to give me a sedative, and I wanted to be nothing but dead. All the while, I kept on muttering incoherent phrases that made sense to no one but me. Words that were circling and pounding in my head like an endless merry-go-round.

I would never get to meet her.

I would never get to meet sweet Cayley.

I would never get to meet my baby girl.

Chapter 30

Nearly a week passed of being back at home, though I wouldn't know it. The minute we returned from the hospital, I wanted to walk right off that cliff again and die. For the first time in my life, I truly believed that there was nothing left for me.

Seth and I hardly spoke at all. With Monty dead and Jane on her way to prison for his murder, all of the dangers that had once surrounded us were gone. No more politics. No more blackmail. No more hideaways.

But what did it matter?

I wanted to have my daughter growing inside my belly.

I wanted to feel her kicking my stomach.

I wanted to hold her in my arms.

Sleep never came to me, and food was even less appealing. I started staying in one of the guest rooms, which I had intended for a nursery, while Seth followed suit and spent each night on the couch downstairs. Sometimes, I wished that he would just stay at his office and never come home. But he showed up every night regardless, perhaps too much of a fool to realize that I was incapable of healing.

As far as grad school was concerned, I decided to take the semester off. Not only did I need to work out the many issues in my life, I needed to get some spark of hope back. I was lost, sad, and alone. Jeremy understood my need for an extended break from waiting tables, but even I started to miss bustling around the kitchen with him while we juggled serving trays on a busy night.

I wanted my own life back. But most of all, I wanted to stop feeling so guilty about it.

I cried every night, wishing that Cabel were here. How I longed to be wrapped up in his arms. From the moment we met, it seemed like we were meant to be.

But none of that mattered now.

He was gone.

My baby was gone.

Maybe I wanted to be gone, too.

* * *

One night, not long after sundown, I left my room and walked past the one Cabel and I used to share. The door was cracked, but when I stopped to open it, everything looked so dark and dreary. The shades were drawn, and I knew that this place must look like a cave in the daytime.

The fact that Seth would no longer sleep in here didn't make much sense to me. Maybe it was because he didn't want to lie in the bed where we used to sleep, the bed where he used to touch me, the bed I always believed that I was sharing with another man. I tried to blink the memory away, but it remained. Whether I liked it or not, the man sleeping downstairs knew me better than anyone else. It was clear that I hardly knew him at all.

My hands were trembling as I crept down the staircase. I had never been so weak in my entire life. I felt cold, and I wasn't hungry. But I trudged towards the kitchen anyway.

The Christmas decorations were still up, though we had never opened presents or even admired them under the tree. I didn't want to touch them because they reminded me of what we once had, of what we would never get back again. Seth slept in the living room among it all every night, and I had no clue how he was able to bear it. Those stockings still hung on the mantle, and I wondered if I had bought one for Cayley, whether or not it would have made any difference.

Once I reached the kitchen, I couldn't remember what I had come down here for. Food was of no interest to me, but my body ached so badly that I decided on a drink of water. Several washed dishes were drying in the drain board, though none belonged to me. I picked up an overturned glass, and it slipped from my hand, shattering into pieces across the floor.

At first, the realization of what had happened did nothing more than startle me. I felt dizzy and useless for not having enough energy to grip an empty glass in my hand. But then I recognized how pathetic and pointless my life had become. Rage overwhelmed me, spreading like an inflamed disease. I was tired of the cards I kept getting dealt and terrified by the reality of never being able to change them. In an instant, something came over me that I could not repress, some manic, raging emotion buried deep within.

I had truly gone mad.

With the swipe of my hand, I batted a stack of dishes across the counter and onto the floor. As they hit the ground with a crash, I knocked over glasses and scattered silverware from every drawer. Then I shoved the contents of the kitchen counter off the surface as each one came toppling to the tile. When I found something else to break, I chucked it across the floor and screamed.

"Finley!" Seth cried, attempting to jerk me out of the line of fire. When I wouldn't budge, he wrapped his arms around my stomach and pulled me away from a bed of shattered glass and porcelain. I bucked against him, but that only made his grip tighten. Imprisoning me in his arms, Seth forced my back against his chest and slammed into the wall, where we slid down to the floor together.

I broke down in tears and hung my head, unable to keep from crying. When I felt his hand on my back, it didn't send the knee-jerk reaction through me that I thought it might. Seth hugged me close and placed his chin over my shoulder, while I relaxed within his hold. It was the first time I had allowed his touch since I discovered who he really was.

"Come back to me, baby."

I felt his breath on my neck, rushing across the surface of my skin like a gust of warm air. He squeezed tight, and I shuddered at the way he made me feel. Like he had been mine all along.

When I leaned my head back to look at him, Seth brushed the hair out of my face and gazed deep into my eyes. I wanted to feel like I could know him, and it suddenly occurred to me that I had. After all, hadn't I been living with this man and sleeping by his side every night for months? He was the same husband, just with a different name.

Feeling as though the weight of the world were on my shoulders, I let my head drop to Seth's chest, and he delicately held me in his arms. We sat on the cold tile floor together for what seemed like hours, while I wept over all that we were and all that we couldn't be.

"Finley," he whispered, stroking his fingers through my hair. "I know how you feel."

"No, you don't," I croaked. My tears dampened his shirt as I sobbed.

He sighed and angled my shoulders so I could look up at him. "You haven't let me explain." His hand reached out to capture mine, and I couldn't deny welcoming the sensation of warmth. "We can't just keep ignoring each other."

Lowering my gaze, I fell limp in his arms and sniffled. "I know."

Seth titled my chin up in the palm of his hand and rubbed his thumb along the length of my jawline. Our eyes met, and I found such a sense of familiarity in those crystal blue spheres that I wanted to forget everything and surrender myself in his arms. But there was that hesitancy, that underlying sense of doubt that held me back every time. How well could I have really known my husband when I didn't even know his own name?

"One day, you're going to have to let me explain," he proposed. "There's no reason why things can't go back to the way they were."

"Don't say that!" I snapped, pulling away from him. But the grip he had on my arms was so tight, that he kept me firmly held within his embrace. "You're a liar! You have no idea how I feel! And— and, Cayley..." I broke down again, spiraling into a fit of emotion. If I didn't stop crying like this, I wouldn't have any energy left to stand.

"Shh..." Seth set my head on his shoulder as I twisted his shirtsleeve in my hand, trying to reconcile with the pain. The physical aspects of losing my daughter were nothing compared to the agony of having my heart split in two.

When Jane pounded those high-heeled spikes into my stomach, she had taken something away from me that I might never have the chance of getting back. But I had blamed Seth for everything regardless. Had he told me who he really was and made me aware of everything that was going on, perhaps I would have been more careful. I might have had the opportunity to take precautions that would ensure our daughter's safety. Now, all I had been left with was no baby, no pregnancy, and an unfamiliar husband.

"I still love you, Finley." Seth's words washed over me with anger and resentment. "If you don't love me anymore, that's okay," he whispered, cupping my cheek in his hand. "But I'm not letting you go. Not until you let me explain." His fingers ghosted along my neck, smoothing and caressing. "But you're not ready for that now."

For the better part of the day, I had been trapped in bed shivering. But as Seth touched my body and held me close, I was actually starting to feel warm. Maybe he would be able to thaw me out in all the places that were frozen. Just like his brother had done before him.

Trusting the man who wore my husband's wedding ring, I let all of the resentment I had been harvesting for him go and relaxed in his embrace. After shutting him out for so long, it felt so good to be held, to cling to the warmth of another human being. When I dozed off, he stood with me in his arms and carried my feeble body upstairs to the bedroom.

In the depth of my subconscious, I longed for him to lay me down on the mattress that we had once shared. My mind had been distracted with anger and pain, but I didn't want the darkness to consume me anymore. Whether I was willing to admit it or not, my body responded to Seth's touch like it had always responded to Cabel's. Perhaps they were one in the same. Or perhaps I really was still in love with my husband after all.

When he opened our bedroom door, I fluttered my eyelashes to observe the place where we used to love and fight. Every argument had always ended here, no matter where it began. I glimpsed the bathroom, where I had locked myself in so many times before, recalling the night Cabel busted the door down. My father had been executed that night, but my husband had taken all of the pain away. I knew that I wanted him to do it again. I knew that he must have been capable of doing it again. Because I had faith in the fantasy that somehow, he might still be the same man.

Seth peeled the covers back and laid me down on the mattress. My arms stayed securely fastened around the back of his neck when he went to stand up, and I couldn't be sure which of us was more stunned by my clingy behavior. He hovered above me, his breath raining over my face in the dark, leaving me breathless and paralyzed beneath him.

"Don't go," I whimpered.

Seth placed his hands on the mattress along either side of my waist. Then he sat down on the edge of the bed and removed my arms from their choke hold around his neck. When his eyes danced across my face, I could feel him pondering the situation.

"Sleep with me," I said, not too ashamed to beg. "Please."

Seth exhaled aloud, then looked me over again. Before I knew it, his fingers were brushing along my face and throat and lips. I lolled my head back and closed my eyes, feeling his thumb skim along the edge of my mouth. But then he stopped, and I blinked up at him in confusion, furrowing my brow. He looked like an angel in the night.

"Don't leave me here by myself," I pleaded, clamping my hand around his arm.

In the end, Seth slipped into bed beside me and lay there without speaking a word. Craving his touch, I wrapped my arms around his torso and returned my head to his chest. There was something so comforting in listening to the beating of his heart, such a sad, familiar rhythm. But when he wouldn't hold me like I wanted him to, like he had in the kitchen downstairs, I felt rejected and unwanted all over again.

When I woke up the next day, Seth was nowhere to be found. The rational side of my brain knew that he had to work, but the emotional side screamed accusations of abandonment. He had left me alone in this, no matter how I pushed him away. Perhaps I wasn't ready to admit that everything was just as much his fault as it was mine.

Chapter 31

For the next month or so, the length of distance that had formed between us widened. He worked all day while I stayed at home in bed, and if anything, the nature of our toxic situation had only gotten worse. I didn't know if I wanted to be married anymore.

It wasn't until March, right on the cusp of Spring Break, that I truly sat down and had a conversation with my husband that lasted more than three minutes. When Seth came home from work, I was sitting on the couch downstairs, where he had reverted to sleeping after that one night we hadn't spent apart. I heard his footsteps in the hall, the click of his keys against the table, and the gasp of astonishment when he entered the living room.

I was holding my head in my hands, sorting through everything that had happened over the past few months. Honestly, I had no idea how I had been able to stand it for this long. Sinking into a deep depression that I had no way of digging myself out of. Living with a man who was as much my husband as he was a stranger. But worst of all, believing that somehow, we could love each other again. I had struggled with the mental, emotional, and psychological turmoil long enough until it became clear to me that there was another way.

Thanks to the practices of our modern era, I didn't have to stay trapped in this semblance of a life if I didn't want to anymore. I was still young, and so was Seth for that matter. There was no need to waste away our lives in misery, clinging to the hope of the way we once were. That was all gone now. When I lost Cayley, I lost everything.

"Finley?" Seth took a few careful steps forward, though not close enough to matter. "Is there something wrong?"

I shook my head and dried my eyes with a tissue, convincing myself that if I could just say what I wanted to, that all of this would be over soon. I could go back to my old apartment, my old life. Or better yet, I could uproot myself and move to a new town, start all over again. It was the fresh start that I had wanted when I moved here in the first place. It was more than just a scholarship that had brought me here for college. I came to this town, so many miles away from home, because I wanted to forget my past. Now that I was older, a grown woman instead of a teenage girl, maybe it would be easier than before.

Lifting my head, I stared into Seth's icy blue eyes and paused. For the first time, I noticed the considerable change in his physical features. Though still as handsome as ever, Seth looked tired, worn out, ragged, as if he had been plagued with an ever-lasting sentence of sleepless nights. I noticed the faint appearance of bruising beneath his eyes and knew that it was all because of me, that this was all my fault.

But then I realized that if we went our separate ways, Seth would have just as much to gain as I would. He could start fresh and have the chance at a new life. Although it made my stomach churn to think of him with another woman, I knew that he must find love with someone else. In spite of everything, surely I owed him that much.

"I don't think I can do this anymore," I confessed.

Seth's eyes widened, and I couldn't tell if it was pain or remorse that had pierced his heart. But I had thought the matter over carefully. In fact, I had been questioning the possibility of our happy lives apart for some time now. Sometimes, separation and divorce aren't selfish. In our case, they were necessary for either of us to go on.

"I've tried and tried, but I just can't." Words left me as I stood up from the couch and walked to the other side of the room with my back to Seth. Maybe if he couldn't see me, see the pained expression on my face, he would be able to understand that I was thinking of the good in it for both of us. I was speaking in the long-term, because I knew that we both deserved to have a future. Even if that meant it was better spent apart.

"If you need help, I can call Dr.—"

"No," I interrupted, feeling my shoulders sag

and heave. "It's not that."

I had been to a therapist more than once. And while those sessions had been beneficial in helping me iron out the issues related to my miscarriage and ultimately, failed pregnancy, there was so much that I hadn't been able to tell her.

The trauma I experienced with Monty and Jane, Blain and Cabel, and now Seth was a series of instances that revolved around terms such as "eye witness" and "evidence." No, I was through with police and investigators, and I had shared with them as little as possible. In the end, they had placed Jane where she belonged, and everyone else was dead.

But what about those of us who had been lucky enough to survive?

I never knew that life would come with such a steep cost. Looking back, I should have known that Jane would win, that she would get what she wanted, because she always did. Even behind the steel bars of a jail cell, she had succeeded in taking my precious little girl from me, sweet baby Cayley, and ruining any chance of a happy marriage as a result.

"I'm talking about us," I whispered.

My heart boomed inside of my chest at the release of those words, and though I could not see the expression on his face, I knew that Seth must have been in pain. But that was all we would ever know if we didn't end this. I couldn't take it anymore.

"No." Seth rushed towards me and grabbed my shoulders, spinning me around to face him. "No. No. No. What do you want me to do? Just tell me how to fix it."

Thickly swallowing, I looked into his eyes and tried to ignore the shaking in my hands. When he cupped my cheek in his palm and brushed his thumb along my wet, tear-stained skin, I opened my mouth and said, "Divorce me."

Seth dropped his hand from my face, backing away from me in shock. Fear flashed across his features, and I hated myself for making him feel that way. Even though he wasn't the man I had believed he was, it was difficult to watch the way pain reshaped his beautiful face into one of anguish and heartbreak.

Seth was still human. Seth was still a man. Seth was still my husband.

While I had rather not admit it, I did love him back then. Maybe I hadn't known who he really was, but I did love him. I loved Cabel. But Cabel was gone.

"So that's it?" He crossed his arms over his chest but stayed where he was. "You just want to quit," he accused with the snap of his fingers. "Just like that."

I gnawed at the edge of my lip. "I've tried. I just can't take it anymore."

Seth nodded and stroked his fingers against his jawline, gazing out the window. Then he turned to the side and scrutinized the Christmas tree that remained in the corner. The one that we had decorated together, back when we were young and in love. A lifetime ago.

"So you want a divorce?" he asked, his voice surprisingly low.

"Yes," I breathed.

Seth walked back over to me with his hands in his pockets. There were tears in my eyes, but he seemed so calm, so cool, so collected. I couldn't imagine how his heart wasn't breaking inside just like mine. But then he looked into my eyes and grasped my arms.

"Do you love me?" Those blue gems did not glance away, though I wished they would.

I pressed my lips together and took a deep breath, letting the tears leak out and stain my cheeks. With some light nodding and an ounce of regret, I muttered, "Yes."

Seth smiled and took my face in his hands, his eyes dancing across mine while I panicked on the inside. I knew what he was going to do before he even did it. But I understood that this may very well be the last time a man I loved held me close, so I let him.

He leaned down and touched his lips to mine, his warm breath rushing in. The tingling of my mouth was as familiar as the chiseled bone structure of his face. When he captured my lower lip between his teeth and tugged, I whimpered at the sensation and fell into his arms. His hands roamed up and down my back, while I twisted my fingers through his hair and kissed him with everything I had in me. But then he lifted the hem of my shirt as he kissed my neck, and the illusion shattered into one harsh reality.

"No!" I moaned, jerking away from him.

Breathless, I turned away so he couldn't see me and held my finger over my lips. That buzzing, electric feeling was there, and I loathed myself for wanting it back. If I knew what was good for me, I would have to fall out of love with Seth. And Cabel.

"I still love you, Finley," Seth murmured. I could feel him drawing near, and when he crept close enough to breathe down my neck, my heart throbbed. "I meant what I said on our wedding day. And I'm not letting you go. Not yet."

Furious at the power he knew he had over me, I spun around to face him and glared. "You think you can just force me to live here with you? When you know I don't want to?"

Seth looked down at me and smirked. "This isn't over between us."

I shoved past him, hissing and snarling as I began to pace the floor.

"You know it isn't," he went on. "So why are you bowing out now?"

My chest rose and fell as I glowered at him from where I stood by the fireplace. After all the pain and hell I had been through, how could he act like this was some competition I had lost? That somehow, we were playing a game, and he was refusing to let me forfeit.

"I don't want to do this anymore," I said through a pair of gritted teeth. "I'm unhappy. You're unhappy. Can't you see how miserable we make each other?"

Seth planted his hands on his hips and looked away, though only for a moment.

"I don't hate you, Seth. But if you make me stay here, I'm going to."

He smoldered at me with the beauty of a burning sun. But then the lightness of his features shifted, and the melancholia went away. "I think that's the first time you've ever said my name. My real name," he noted, the edge of his mouth lifting at the corner.

Tears stung my eyes, and I was so tired of fighting.

"What do you want from me, Seth?" I shook my head at him. "Huh?"

He furrowed his brow, pouting in a manner that drew attention to those full, lush lips.

"What do you want from me?" I screamed, nearly about to rip my hair out by the roots.

As I sat down on the couch and balled my eyes out, Seth took a seat beside me, laying his arm over my shoulder. When he pulled me close, I didn't resist. Instead, I surprised myself by crying in his arms, merely because there was no one else around to empathize with me.

"All right." Seth patted my back and tucked my head beneath his chin. "If it makes you that unhappy, then we'll get a divorce."

Stunned by the nature of his words, I withdrew from him immediately, thinking I had heard him wrong. Surely, he was too much of a man to quit so easily. Was he really willing to let me go without a fight? I was disappointed, because I didn't want him to.

"Really?" I mouthed, hardly able to believe it myself. He was giving me what I wanted, what I had suggested, what I had asked for, so why did I feel so nauseous?

"Yes," he succumbed. "But you have to do something for me first."

"Okay." I batted my lashes and regarded him with interest. "What?"

"I rented a house in the mountains for a week," he began, while I sank into the couch with equal remorse and regret. "I thought it would do you good to get out of town for a while." He took my hand in his and said, "I thought it would do us both good."

"Why didn't you tell me?" I wondered.

"It was going to be a surprise." He stared at the ground and shrugged indifferently. "I guess it doesn't matter now. Does it?"

When he glanced over his shoulder at me, I didn't know what to say.

"What do you want me to do, Seth?"

He let go of my hand and rose from the couch, leaving me to sit alone. "Come with me. It's only for a week," he explained, "over Spring Break."

Before I could respond, he shoved his hands in his pockets and failed to make eye contact. "When we get back, if you still want the divorce, I'll give it to you. Whether I want to or not."

Squirming on the couch, I tried to find reason in the matter and even twiddled my thumbs. But I couldn't come to a decent conclusion. So I asked, "Why do you want to spend a week with me? Wouldn't you rather go on vacation by yourself?"

Seth cleared his throat and flicked his crystal eyes up to meet mine. "You're still my wife. Aren't you?" he questioned, perplexing me beyond belief.

"Yes."

"Well, maybe I want to spend as much time with you as I can. Even if it's only for a little while. I know I can't make you love me again, but I can at least try."

In that moment, something clicked inside of my head, though he began to walk away. Suddenly, I understood why everything felt so wrong, why my mind was demanding that I flee, while my heart was begging me to stay. How had I been so foolish?

"I'll go on one condition," I claimed.

Seth stopped in his tracks, looking me over with wonder and intrigue.

"What?" He lifted his shoulders, and I spotted the desperate ray of hope in his eyes.

"You have to tell me everything," I insisted. "Who you really are. Why you lied to me. Why you married me. Why you've been pretending to be Cabel and for how long."

Seth stared into my eyes without blinking as I rose to stand in front of him.

"I want to know everything," I demanded. "Promise that you'll tell me. It's the only way I'll agree to go." I wrapped my arms around my stomach and hugged my childless frame.

"Okay," he accepted, calm and reticent. "I promise."

"You promise what?" I snapped, questioning whether or not I could trust his word.

Seth pursed his lips and then said, "I promise to tell you everything."

"You can't lie to me anymore," I whispered, my voice sullen and shaky.

"I know that. And I'm sorry. I'm so sorry for everything."

I couldn't imagine how he thought that those few words were enough to atone for all the damage he had done. As tears filled my eyes again, I recognized the difference between these hot, angry drops and the warm, sad moisture that had drizzled down my cheeks earlier. I didn't know how we could fix this. But if he was willing to try, then I was, too.

"So am I." I stepped away from Seth and fled the room, even though he had reached out for me, even though he was still calling my name. Racing up the staircase, I reverted to my old coping mechanism and locked myself in the bathroom.

As the tub filled with water, I observed my naked body in the mirror. I was pale and thin and skin and bones, covered in freckles and goosebumps. When I placed my hand over my stomach, I recalled the slight belly that had once been there and knew how badly I wanted it back. Of all my fears, being unable to carry another child was the greatest.

Chapter 32

The sound of gravel crunching beneath the tires seemed to anchor me as Seth pulled up to a beautiful mountain home with rustic architecture and a riverside view. The two-story structure was secluded from the rest of the rental property, alluding to the time I had spent with Cabel in that cabin in the woods all those years ago. I wondered if Seth had chosen this location for a reason, or if he was still longing to give me the honeymoon we had never had. Surely, his last attempt had been dangerous enough.

After unloading the car, I followed Seth up the front steps and entered our home for the next seven days. The scent of juniper and pine rushed over me, as I walked through the foyer and explored the first floor on my own, trudging through the kitchen, living room, and hallways attached. When I returned to the main area, I opened the French doors and ambled out onto the deck, taking in the glorious wealth of trees all around us. Through the lofty branches, I could glimpse the running rapids of the river down below, while an army of mountains completed the picture-perfect landscape up above, where the clear blue sky reached down to meet the smoky tops of every peak.

"What do you think?" Seth snuck up behind me on the deck, nearly taking my breath away. I kept my eyes on the scenery ahead, unable to grant him the satisfaction of startling me. He may have brought me here, but that didn't mean I had to enjoy it.

"I need to unpack." I turned around and shoved past him, our shoulders brushing in the process. Once I strode into the house, Seth followed me like a dog at my heels.

"The bedroom is upstairs," he informed, shutting and locking the French doors behind us. His footsteps came closer to me when I had yet to move, and I wondered if I could stay put forever.

"Really?" I glanced up at him with aggravation, clutching my luggage in my hands. The straps over one suitcase were digging into my shoulder, but I wasn't about to ask him for help. "You're telling me that this place only has one bedroom?"

He rocked forward on the tips of his toes, his hands artfully placed at either of his hips. "Yep," he announced, popping the 'p' in his pronunciation of the word, just to be obnoxious.

Huffing in frustration, I made my way up the wooden staircase to find a cozy master bedroom with a large bed, fine furniture, a walk-in bathroom, and a round window overlooking the breathtaking view of the mountains and forest surrounding us. For the first time since I had lost the baby, I felt safe, tucked away in the woods where no one could find us. I wished that I could have been myself again, that Seth could have been the Cabel I had known, that we could have taken this trip as soon as we got married, not months later when there was hardly anything left of a marriage between us.

"What would you like to do first?" Seth appeared in the room, taking me by surprise yet again. I tossed my heavy luggage onto the mattress and scowled, tired of his lingering presence everywhere I went. I had signed up for this trip for one reason and one reason only: to find out exactly who he was and why I had never known. As soon as I knew the truth and those seven days were up, I was headed home with plans for an amicable divorce.

Ignoring Seth, I sprung up and tossed myself across the bed, landing on an empty space of comfort amongst all the luggage. The spontaneous act made me feel like a child again, so I threw my head back with laughter, closing my eyes in bliss. As I relaxed and began to feel truly content, the aching affliction in my body seemed to momentarily subside.

"Okay then. We'll sleep."

My eyelids slid open at the sound of Seth's unusually chipper voice. Disappointed, I sat up on my elbows and watched him take my suitcase and other bags off the bed and stow them away in the closet. Then he shut the door and sailed into the air, landing on the mattress beside me. When I scoffed at his behavior, Seth merely lay back and slipped his hands behind his head, shutting his crystalline eyes with a clever smirk on his face.

"What do you think you're doing?"

Seth drummed his fingers over his chest and chuckled, then smiled up at me and rolled onto his side. He rested his head in the palm of his hand, studying the look of scrutiny on my face. I saw passion and lust in his eyes, but wanted nothing of it.

"We're on our second honeymoon," he declared, twirling a piece of my hair.

"No, we're not." I leaned forward on my knees and batted his hand away.

The expression on Seth's face vanished, but I was determined to stand my ground.

"I don't even know who you are," I snipped. "And I did not come here to have fun."

As I moved to slide down off the bed, Seth grabbed my wrist and yanked me back. Before I knew it, I was sinking into the mattress, helplessly pinned beneath him. He held my arms over my head and lowered his face above mine, his hot breaths quick and harsh.

"You think I don't hate myself every day for what happened? You think I don't wish that I could take it back? Everything. All of it," he rasped, his blue eyes sharp and alert.

While I could have bucked against him in an

attempt to wiggle free, I lay still, even though the submissive reaction came as a shock to me. After nearly three months of not being touched, it was the closest I had gotten to my husband making love to me.

"I miss her too, Finley. But I still have you."

I took a deep breath, never letting my gaze shift from his eyes.

"And you still have me. Why can't you see that?"

There were veins throbbing in Seth's neck, and all of the blood was rushing to his head. But there was something so desperate, so human in his words, that I felt my insides slowly beginning to melt at the feel of his breath on my neck. Even now, I still wanted him.

"You're tearing us apart, and it's killing me." He swallowed, moistening his lips before exhaling in a way that made every inch of my skin tingle. "I want you, Finley. Now more than ever." His mouth hovered dangerously close to mine. "I want every part of you, every piece. I want you every night and day. But I want you to want me back. Like you used to."

Feeling the sweet warmth in my blushing cheeks, I parted my lips to say his name.

But he cut me off and confessed, "I want you to love me again."

"Seth—"

"Just try," he begged, his body heat all around me. "Just try to love me again."

His mouth claimed mine, and I gasped at the sudden impact of his crushing lips. Desire awakened within the depth of my soul, blooming and spreading, while warm blood began to pound and pulse through my veins. Seth rested his knee between my legs and urgently worked his mouth against mine, as if he were trying to suck every last breath out of me.

"Seth," I rasped, alive with fire at the way he was making me feel.

His hand slid over my jeans as he curled my leg around his hip, dragging my body closer to his. I hardly had time to come up for air until his lips traveled the length of my neck, sucking and nipping at my skin. He tugged at the hem of my shirt and swiftly pulled the fabric over my head, while I harbored no intentions of stopping him.

When he left a trail of kisses from my neck to my collarbone, I tilted my head back and sighed in the wish of allowing him easier access to my throat. Once he released my arms, his hands smoothed along either side of my torso, his bare skin against mine. Then his palms sank into the small of my back as his mouth danced across my ribcage, leaving kisses all along my naked flesh. My fingers tangled through his hair when the tip of his finger traced that fine line between my breasts. I felt his knuckles against my sternum and the stubble of his beard against my stomach, as I willingly let my guard down.

"Cabel," I sighed, lost in touch and emotion.

Within an instant, Seth reared back on the bed, and the whole moment was over. I opened my eyes with a furrowed brow, then suddenly recalled what I had just said. Though I had used the wrong name, he had been the one to convince me that it was the right one. Shouldn't he have been apologizing for lying to me in the first place? How could he expect me to be anything but confused? The only man's name I'd ever uttered in bed was Cabel's.

But as I gazed into his eyes, willing him to continue, I knew that our chance of restoring love and trust between us had ended for the night. He crawled away from me and sat on the edge of the bed, running his fingers through his golden hair. I shivered at the rejection and put my shirt back on, too offended and miserable to stay in here with him any longer.

"I'm sorry," I muttered, though there should have been no need for an apology.

Seth lifted his head and exhaled, but showed no intention of resuming his advances upon me. So I left the room as quickly as possible and barreled down the staircase. Once I was alone in the kitchen, I sank down to the floor and cried tears of thwarted affection and serious, heart-sweltering remorse.

Chapter 33

My heart was breaking all over again, because my husband didn't want me. He didn't long for my touch the way I desperately desired his. He didn't need to feel my body clinging to him as badly as I wanted his body wrapped around mine. In spite of everything, I missed his touch, the touch of the man I had married, whoever he was. Whether he had lied to me or not, I knew that he must still pine for me in some fashion or form. If not, then seven days in a beautiful home in the mountains was nothing but pure torture.

"Okay," Seth spoke. Once again, I hadn't heard him come in.

Collecting myself up off the floor, I clutched the edge of the countertop to steady my shaky posture and felt a pulsing quickness in my hands. I leaned against the stove and appreciated the fact that my back was to him, so he couldn't see that he had hurt me again. A shiver crept down my spine, as I threaded my fingers through my hair and smeared the back of my hands over my tears. Before I had the chance to turn around, he spoke again.

"I'll tell you the truth," he silently declared. "I'll tell you whatever you want to know."

Amazed at his sudden acquiescence, I looked back over my shoulder at the man I hardly knew. But the minute our eyes connected, he took a few steps away from me and began pacing the floor. I couldn't understand why he was willing to relinquish his side of the bargain so early on, as it was only Sunday, the first day of the week. If he revealed everything to me now, surely I could just pack my bags and leave, ruining his attempt at a romantic getaway, our last trip together as husband and wife.

"Okay," I accepted, nodding in agreement.

When I took his hand, Seth stilled at the touch, but I dragged him into the living room anyway. He plopped down on the sofa, perhaps believing that I might join him. But I had already decided how things were going to be if I agreed to hear and keep all of his dirty little secrets for him. I would have to be someone other than the woman who loved him.

"What do you want to know, Finley?" he asked, impatient and curt.

I trudged over to the French doors and peered through the glass at the remaining tinges of dusk. We had barely missed the sunset, and it made me feel sad. I had been floundering through life over the past several weeks, helplessly missing everything. Now, I realized that I should have made better use of the time we had together.

Maybe that was why he had taken me to that resort on the beach for Christmas. Because he knew that the clock was ticking. That these moments would soon fade to dust.

"What is your real name?" I hovered towards the empty fireplace, the cool stone artfully designed and aesthetically intended for a place like this. It was spring now, so there was no need for the warmth. But I didn't want to feel like the leftover logs on the rack. Something misplaced and ignored for the time being, simply because there was no use for them anymore. I didn't want the flames to burn out and leave me in the cold.

"Seth Jones."

"No." I shook my head. "Your full name."

He swallowed and placed his hands in his lap. "Seth Avery Jones."

"Avery?" I echoed, a delightful chime to my voice.

"Yeah. It was my grandfather's name."

"Hmm..." I didn't know what to do with that answer. "Who is Cabel Jones?"

He straightened his posture, and I hated the fact that this felt like a court room.

"My twin brother," he clipped, casting his eyes down.

"Who's the oldest?"

"I am."

"By how much?"

He stroked the stubble of his beard and relinquished, "A minute or so."

I chewed on my lip, wishing that I had a pen in my hand to click. Anything to let me move my body and limbs until I had worked all the nervous energy out of my system.

"Were you close?" I walked in a straight line on the tips of my toes.

"When we were kids I guess," he faded out, so I waited for him to continue.

But then he didn't, so I muttered, "What happened?"

"I don't know." He shrugged his shoulders. "We never had that much in common."

"Really?" I glowered at him, not liking the irony one bit.

"That's not what I mean," he argued. "Cabel was just so different from me. We're not anything alike. Yes, we were identical. I get that. But there wasn't anything else."

"Anything else what?" I demanded, aggravated that he kept dropping off.

"We're just entirely different people. That's all I meant."

I exhaled through my nostrils and ran my palms over the tops of my arms, wondering how I would ever make it through the length of this interrogation. My eyes flicked to the high ceilings and wooden beams overhead, while I recognized the room as nothing more than the setting for a modern day Spanish Inquisition. I didn't want to question my husband and unravel every secret and lie that he had used to mask the truth. But he had finally given me a chance at honesty. So I had to.

"What were you like as a teenager?"

Either corner of his mouth lifted at the question. "Normal, I guess."

I braided my fingers together behind my back and searched the burgundy rug over the hardwood floor. The thought had occurred to me that I could ask a few meaningless questions like this, merely for the sake of prolonging the inevitable. Deep down, I didn't want to know the person my husband really was. What if I didn't like him?

"I played baseball," he added, his eyes bright and shining.

Intrigued at the idea, I eyed his figure from head to toe and imagined the teenage jock who used to fill his shoes. Images flashed through my mind of fresh cut grass, team jerseys, and baseball gloves. I could only imagine what the girls must have been like during Seth's adolescence, swooning at the sheer sight of him. The golden boy at seventeen.

"Did you date much?" I prodded. "How many girlfriends did you have?"

He massaged his knuckles with his fingers and sighed, "A couple."

My eyes widened at the confession, as I stared down at him in horror.

"Not at the same time," he defended. "What kind of guy do you think I am?"

"Sorry. I just," I hesitated, searching for the right words, "didn't know."

He knitted his eyebrows together and gazed up at me, clearly offended and hurt.

"How old are you?"

He blinked twice at the question then answered. "Twenty-eight."

I set my hands on my hips and started pacing again. "When is your birthday?"

"June seventh," he replied, relaxing into the sofa with a comfortable look on his face.

I stood in place for a moment, remembering the days when I had been interested in astrology and horoscopes. Those born between the twenty-first of May and the twenty-first of June would be forever marked with all traits of a Gemini. The corresponding Zodiac symbol for that particular time of the year was twins, and I shivered at the irony.

"What is it?" Seth looked concerned, his facial features etched with worry.

"You're a Gemini," I noted. "The twins. It's just funny is all."

"Then why aren't you laughing?" His husky blue eyes met mine as I lost the ability to smile. "Why do I get the feeling that these aren't the questions you should be asking?"

"Because they aren't," I brusquely replied. "The truth is I don't know what to ask you."

"Yes you do." Seth straightened his posture and rested his arm along the back of the couch. "I know what you want. You're just too afraid to ask me for it."

"What do I want then?" I challenged, cocking my head to the side at him.

"You want to know how long I've pretended to be Cabel and not Seth. You want to know which one of us loved you. And you want to know why we did it. Am I right?"

I pressed my lips together, unable to look away. "Yes."

"Ask me then," he urged, growing impatient. "Do it."

Surprising him and even myself, I turned the tables and posed an unexpected question next. My hands were trembling as I asked, "Did you sleep with her? With Jane?"

Seth looked me in the eye and scoffed. "I never touched her. Jane was Cabel's girlfriend, not mine. I only knew about her because he told me."

"But," I rubbed my thumb against my lower lip. "I thought that—"

"She's someone from his past, not mine," he reinforced. "I'm sorry I never told you."

Stumbling through all the confusion, I collected my wits and felt my temples begin to throb with tension and stress. "So when did you switch? Why did you—?"

"Cabel used to get in trouble a lot," he said. "And when we were kids, Blain would pick on him and beat him up all the time. Our parents didn't care. They said it would teach him a lesson. So I started switching places with him. I'd wear his clothes and he'd wear mine. I thought it would be better if Blain beat me instead. I was the one who could handle it."

I fluttered my lashes several times and sat down on the love seat across from him. "How long did that go on? The two of you switching places like that?"

"At first, it was every now and then." Seth draped one leg over the other, resting his right ankle over his left thigh. "But by the time we started college, we were practically switching all the time. I got so used to being called Cabel. Before I knew it, it was every day."

I ground my teeth together and exhaled aloud, trying to put the pieces into place. "I don't understand," I breathed. "Why would you keep switching places?"

Seth curled his index finger and set it between his lips, distracting me so effortlessly. I wanted his mouth on mine, but I couldn't lose focus. Not now.

"Well, we went to Northwestern together and then Johns Hopkins and Cornell after that. We had the same major, the same classes. It was easier to keep people from noticing. Cabel started dating Jane, and I hardly saw him at all. Then he came to me one day and said that he was dropping out of grad school. He wanted to switch places permanently, so I agreed."

"But why?" I shook my head from side to side, drowning in frustration. "At that point, what were you protecting him from?" I rested my chin in the palm of my hand.

Seth smoldered, a gorgeous golden boy look that had always sent my heart racing with desire. It had the same effect tonight, though I was bewildered and perplexed.

"Cabel kept threatening to tell the press Blain's secret."

"What? About him being born in Greece?"

"Yes," Seth hissed. "Cabel always held it over his head. He thought that he could get back at Blain for torturing him as a child. So when it came time for Blain to run for president, they came looking for me instead of Cabel."

"Because they thought you were Cabel," I assumed.

"Yes." He leaned forward and set his elbow over his knees, watching me.

"But why would you do that? Let Cabel use you like that?" I got up from the couch and walked in front of the window. "He knew they would be after you." I turned on my heel to glance back at him, as the wheels kept turning in my head. "He knew they would kill you."

"I know." He rubbed his hands together and lifted his head to look up at me.

I grimaced as if I had just tasted something foul. "But why?"

"Because he was my brother, Finley. And I protect the people I care about."

I thought of a painful response that was below the belt, but kept it inside.

"In the end, it didn't matter anyway." He scratched the back of his head and then folded his arms across his chest. "By then, Blain already knew what we were doing."

A thousand occurrences flitted across my mind. Suddenly, it all made sense.

"I wouldn't have minded taking the fall for him, but then I met you."

I held my hand over my mouth in astonishment, still trying to reckon with what I had just realized.

"The only reason I didn't let them take me, the only reason I even tried to escape was because of you." He rose from the couch and moved towards me. "I didn't want anything to happen to you. You had nothing to do with any of it, Finley. You didn't know."

"So the first time I met Cabel, the real Cabel—"

"You only saw him one time," Seth finished. "He died in your arms."

"So that day in the rain." I paused to take a breath. "When I first saw Cabel."

"That was me," he proclaimed. "It's been me the whole time."

I twisted my fingers through my hair as my head began to spin. My throat felt very dry and my breathing grew louder and sharper. I must have been having a nervous breakdown.

Seth clasped my hand and placed it over his heart. "The only difference is my name."

I splayed my fingers across my throat and

started to cry. It was too much.

"I've been myself with you the whole time, Finley. I'm the one who was your professor. I'm the one who took you to the cabin. I'm the one who fell in love with you." He took my face in his hands and swiped his thumbs beneath my eyes where fresh tears were collecting. "I'm the one who married you. And I'm the one who can't live without you."

I hung my head and sobbed, grasping his wrists for support. Somehow, it was a miracle the way my wildest dreams had come true. The Cabel I had known and loved was right here before my very eyes. He hadn't died in my arms all those years ago. He hadn't left me to unknowingly marry his twin brother instead. It had been him all along. But the relief and shock fused together to form doubt and disbelief. It was too good to be true.

"You promise that this is real?" I wept, so close to his face. "You promise that you're not lying this time? That you're telling the truth?"

"I told you that it was still me on New Year's Eve. You just didn't believe me."

"But how do I know that it's really you? How do I know?" I couldn't accept it, because I wanted so badly for it to be true. It would break my heart if it wasn't.

"You're just going to have to believe me," he crooned, pressing his forehead to mine.

With a mournful sigh, I whimpered, "I don't know if I can."

Just like that, I withdrew from him and ran, scrambling up the staircase.

Chapter 34

I wrestled with the covers and tangled the sheets, as the next several hours turned into a sleepless night. Despite the warm blankets all around me, I couldn't escape the sensation of feeling cold. So I tossed and turned, eventually lying awake to stare through the window at the moon and stars. My mind had yet to stop racing, and I was unavoidably restless.

Wrapped in the duvet, I sauntered downstairs and found Seth on the couch in the living room. My footsteps were mildly loud at best, as I crept towards him in the night. Despite everything he had once hidden from me and now revealed, I missed the comfort of his body lying next to me. No matter the situation, I wanted my husband back.

"What are you doing down here, Finley?" he grumbled, though his eyes were still closed. I admired his beautiful face from afar, the way the shadows played over his features.

"I'm cold," I confessed, quiet and subtle. As I slipped closer and sat down on the arm of the sofa, Seth jerked the one blanket he had away to expose his bare, chiseled torso.

"So what do you want me to do about it?" He combed his fingers through his hair and sat up straight, yawning and stretching in the moonlight.

While I appreciated his acceptance of my need for space, I couldn't help feeling disappointed when he didn't come to bed. In time, I would believe him and all the things he had said. But I couldn't wrap my head around the insanity of it all in one night.

"I don't like sleeping alone," I said, aiming to persuade him into coming upstairs.

"You could have fooled me," he quipped. Then he chuckled and sighed.

Dropping down onto the couch cushion beside him, I took his hand in mine and circled my thumb across the center of his palm. I heard the quickness of breath in his voice at my touch, and the sound filled my spirit with hope. When he turned his head to the side and looked at me, I licked my lips and swallowed, wondering if he would touch me.

Seth stood up instead and pulled me to my feet. "Come on," he murmured, braiding his fingers with mine. "Let's get you to bed."

My insides swirled into a pool of happiness as he led me up the staircase. Once we entered the room, I climbed onto the bed and stretched out beneath the covers. Seth waited for a moment before joining me under them, keeping a sliver of space between us. I rebelled against the minimal distance and placed my hand over his chest.

"Finley," Seth growled, lifting my hand off his torso. "You can't keep teasing me like this. You either want me or you don't. Stop torturing me."

"I'm not torturing you." I leaned forward and reclined on my elbows. When he looked at me, I couldn't be sure whether his arctic blue eyes truly belonged to the man I had known or I just wanted them to. But desire was unfurling in the depth of my belly, as the warmth began to spread.

"Then what are you doing?" He reached his hand out to touch my face, then pulled away, struggling with doubt. "I've already told you the truth. I've told you everything."

"I know you have," I breathed, wanting him to hold me. "But you're just going to have to give me some time to process all of this. It's a lot to take in all at once."

Seth placed his palm to the side of my face, and I shuddered at the touch. With his fingers in my hair and his thumb against my cheek, I wanted nothing more than to let it go. To believe everything he had told me and take his word for it, no matter how confusing or perplexing or mind-boggling it all was. It wasn't like what he had said was impossible. Improbable, maybe. But it was definitely possible. Maybe it was true.

"Okay," Seth relented, clutching my fingers in his hand. "I understand."

As he lay back down and put his head on the pillow, I watched him relax and smiled with relief.

Once he closed his eyes, I reclined on my side of the bed and rolled onto my stomach to acknowledge his presence. Feeling him here beside me felt like such a huge step for the two of us. So I tucked my hands beneath my pillow and observed him in the night, the way he slept, the way he inhaled, the way he breathed. When it seemed safe to do so, I inched my way towards his body and rested my head on his chest.

I could feel him stirring awake, but I was not going anywhere. My arm went around his waist, while I hugged him close and shut my eyes. Seth cleared his throat and then placed his hand on my back, accepting the closeness I wanted, while at the same time recognizing the intimacy that we had both been living without.

Comfortable in his arms, I nuzzled his chest and traced patterns in his skin with my fingers. So maybe I was being unfair, teasing and torturing him. But he easily drifted off, gently snoring beneath me. Thrilled at the sound, I listened to his heartbeat and each intake of breath into his lungs. Seth may have been a man filled with secrets and lies, merely conjured to protect his selfish fool of a twin brother, Cabel. Regardless, he looked the same, he talked the same. Maybe he was the same.

Either way, he was all mine.

Chapter 35

By Wednesday, Seth and I had settled into a comfortable vacation in the mountains. For the past two days, we had ventured out into the wilderness of a world surrounding us, taking long hikes and sorting through the confusing mess that was our life. In those moments, I let him take my hand and guide me through the woods. For me, the gesture signaled one game-changing truth—that I was willing to try.

When I woke up that morning, Seth was laying there with his arms crossed over his chest, looking straight ahead. I shifted beneath the covers and gazed over at him, unsure of what he was thinking. There was a frown on his face that curved either side of his mouth at the corners. Somehow, it made him look pretty.

"Hey," I whispered, pressing my cheek into the pillow. "What's wrong?"

"Nothing," he clipped, short and abrasive.

I sat up in the bed and watched him peel the covers back, stomping off to the bathroom. When he slammed the door behind him, I flinched, not knowing what I could have done to set him off.

Even though we were sharing the same bed, Seth had yet to touch me since I had uttered his brother's name. In all honesty, I wasn't sure if I wanted him to.

So he made breakfast for me, even though he hated to cook, and I had to admire him for that. I didn't know what he wanted from me, because I had no clue how to make this man happy. After all, the whole time I had known him, Seth was pretending to be somebody else.

Our morning ended on a scenic bike trail, and when we made it back to the house, I took a shower alone. I kept trying to convince myself that Seth was the same man I had fallen in love with and married. He was my husband.

But it all seemed too good to be true.

* * *

For lunch, we had smoked barbeque, and I couldn't believe that he had gone so far as to fire up the grill. Complete with baked beans and leftover potato salad from the fridge, the meal truly felt like comfort food. Maybe this was what it tasted like to be home. I'd never had a family, but maybe Seth could be mine.

Maybe he already was.

Later that afternoon, Seth wanted to take me out on the river. It was bright outside, and I knew the sunshine would be warm. But there was so much unresolved tension between us that I didn't know what to do.

"Did you bring a bathing suit?"

"Yeah," I replied, noticing that he was already wearing his. "I did."

The way he paced the floor in our bedroom reminded me so much of Cabel. But then I realized that he was Cabel. That the Seth I had known was the same Cabel I had known. His mannerisms were the same. His reactions. His emotions. His charm.

The only difference was his name.

Try as I might, it was too difficult to wrap my head around. Ever since we met, everything became so sudden and dangerous and alarming. I wanted to go back to the naïve nineteen-year-old I had once been, but I just couldn't.

Maybe if he touched me... only there was fear there, too. Fear that this man with a different name wouldn't love me the same. And yet, he had been the same all along. I was hopeless and stressed, still upset about losing the baby. I felt broken on the inside, like damaged goods. What if I couldn't give either of us what we wanted anymore?

"The water should be nice," he predicted, his eyes on my back as I rifled through my suitcase in the closet.

"I'm sure it is, Seth." I hung my head and sighed. The only bathing suit I had packed was a hot pink string bikini.

My mind flashed back to a time when Cabel and I had been so hopelessly in love. I didn't know if we would be able to get that back again.

The girl who used to wear that hot pink bikini lived and breathed Cabel Jones. But I wasn't that girl anymore.

"You don't have to say it like that."

"Say what?" I turned around and glared.

"My name," he barked, planting his hands on his hips. "You don't have to say it like I'm some stranger."

"Well, you are," I declared, snatching the bikini out of my suitcase. When I brushed past him to go change in the bathroom, he grabbed my arm and pulled me back.

"No, I'm not," he growled. "I'm your husband."

"Not for long," I muttered under my breath.

Seth gritted his teeth and stared down at me, his fingers digging into my arm as he smoldered. "What? What are you saying?"

"I don't know." I jerked myself out of his grasp and stood by the bed. "I don't know what I'm saying." I gazed out the window and clutched the bikini to my chest. "I haven't decided yet."

I felt his breath on my neck as he lingered behind me. "Finley, I—"

"Will you just go so I can change?" I snapped, turning my head to the side while at the same time refusing to look back at him.

"I'm sorry, I—"

"Just go!" I shut my eyes tight, because there were tears spilling down from them.

I heard soft footsteps and then the door shut.

Rushing to the bathroom, I splashed cool water on my face from the sink and then tied my hair back into a loose ponytail. I stripped my clothes off and put the bathing suit on, surprised by how tightly I had to tie the strings.

Gawking at my frail, thin body in the mirror, I couldn't believe how fragile my frame had become. While I had only just gotten my appetite back this week, I couldn't believe that I still looked so small. No wonder Seth had started cooking. He was trying to put some meat on my bones. Only now I understood how badly I needed fattening up.

Self-conscious, I pulled a cover-up over my head and trudged downstairs to join my husband. When he wasn't there, I walked out onto the deck and found him waiting for me. His seamlessly perfect body was on full display, his tan skin and blonde hair even more so from all the time in the sun. While his chiseled chest and abs were model-worthy, and the muscle tone in his arms hinted at great physical strength, my head was cloudy again. And when my thoughts became so muddled that I could hardly think, I just wanted to get in the water.

"You need some?" Seth held up a bottle of sunscreen, SPF 30. "I'll put it on for you."

"No," I said when he twisted the cap off. "I'm fine."

While I may have been fair-skinned and freckled, my body was not prepared to have his hands rubbing lotion all over me. I had yet to come to terms with everything he had revealed to me on our first night here. Part of me felt like an adulteress, cheating on Cabel with his twin brother. Maybe Seth had told me so many lies that I just couldn't believe the truth.

Feeling daring out in the sunlight, I stripped my cover-up off and tossed it at Seth. Then I raced down the steps and through the grass on my bare feet until I reached the river. There was a black inner tube waiting for me on the bank that Seth must have retrieved from the shed on the property. So I grabbed the donut-shaped float and stepped into the water, sitting down at the open space in the middle.

Seth waded into the river and swam up beside me, grabbing one of the handles on the float to stay by my side. I leaned back on the inner tube and closed my eyes, feeling the warm sun on my skin. Though I could feel him watching me, I wanted nothing more than to bask in the daylight while he admired what he had once had so firmly held within the palm of his hand. I lingered near the house, careful not to drift off too far, as my husband remained unavoidably close by.

"So, do you like it out here?" Seth wondered, glued to my side.

"Yeah, I do." A smile graced my lips though I failed to open my eyes. I was trying to relax, regardless of the circumstances. I didn't have much to say.

"Finley, there are so many things that I've wanted to tell you."

I dipped my feet in the water and sighed. "You can tell me later."

"But I want to tell you now," he pushed, furthering my frustration.

"And I want a marriage that wasn't built on a lie," I retorted.

Only Seth didn't think it was very funny.

He waited a beat and then said, "I was protecting you, too."

"Really, how?" I fluttered my lashes and tilted my head back with vanity.

Seth groaned aloud. "Can't you just give me a chance?" He touched my elbow, but I jerked my arm away. "If the roles were reversed, I would do the same for you."

"Sure," I droned, scoffing at the ridiculous remark that meant nothing.

"You know what I think?" he accused, taking a defensive tone with me.

"What?" I snapped, though I could care less which thoughts had been swimming around in his mind.

"I think you don't want this marriage to work," he claimed. "It doesn't matter what I do. You're still going to pick me apart in the end."

A moment of silence passed between us, as I tried to decide whether or not he was right. Honestly, he was pushing me too hard, too fast. I was trying to accept this new life, where I had no child and my husband had a new name. How could he expect me to take all of this in over a few days? I was only human.

"Finley?" His voice sounded sharp and lacked a good dose of patience.

"What?" I snipped, angry with him for turning my rejuvenation period into a heated argument. The river should have been an oasis for the relaxation of my body and mind.

"What do you want?" He posed the question, and I misunderstood him at once. Shouldn't I have been the one confused over his needs and desires? Seth was the spouse who had voluntarily decided to bring me into a life of deception and lies, not me.

I opened my eyes and straightened my posture to scrutinize him in the bright light. If I had been wearing a pair of sunglasses, I would have snatched them off and gotten in his face just to prove a point. He had been a fool to expect acceptance and understanding from me overnight.

"I don't know yet," I argued, loathing the high pitched nature of my voice, the way it scratched and wavered when I yelled. "What?" My throat felt sore already, but I wasn't about to back down. "Are you that afraid that I'm going to leave you?"

But then he beat me to it and went straight for the jugular.

"You've already done it once," he reasoned, flicking his wet tongue out to moisten his lips. The sound of the river flowing left me feeling numb, especially since his shadow and reflection danced across the water. I studied the beautiful man I saw and wondered how nature's representation could hold more promise than the original.

Seth held my gaze and then looked off, his head hanging low.

His words stung, because it showed how little faith he had in me. But shouldn't it have been the other way around? He was the one with a false identity who had been lying to me.

I slid off the inner tube and pushed it away from me, then touched my feet to the ground. Fuming with rage, I slapped my hand across his liquid portrait in the water so it splashed Seth directly in the face. The harsh impact must have stung, but I didn't care. I wanted to hurt him like he had hurt me. When he dragged the back of his hands over his eyes, I was surprised by how much it upset me. I didn't want to see him in discomfort or pain. Maybe we weren't right for each other. We had been once, but we weren't anymore.

In a hurry to get out of the river, I scrambled towards the edge and tripped, scraping the side of my leg on a stone. Air passed through my teeth as I hissed with the pain. By the time I climbed up the river bank, a thin stream of blood was running down my ankle.

"Finley!" Seth appeared at my heels as I winced, hobbling through the grass.

"Calm down. I'm fine," I declared, aggravated and tense.

"No, you're not." He snatched me up and carried me into the house in his arms.

"Seth," I whined, wanting to be free of this man. My husband.

But he ignored my complaints and headed up the staircase until we reached the master bathroom. It was unwanted and unnecessary, the way he worried over something as minor as a bloody cut from a river rock. When he set me down on the counter by the sink, I knew better than to run away from him. Maybe Seth thought that if he mended a wound or two, the doctoring would serve as penance for all the damage he had done.

Damage that he couldn't take back.

"Why is it always the right side?" Seth wiped the blood away and cleaned the gash in my leg. Catching on to his comment, I examined the injury, realizing for the first time that it was not that far away from my once broken foot. That felt like a million years ago.

Furrowing my brow, I recalled the time he had re-broken the places in my foot before they healed improperly. Sitting here by the sink also reminded me of the night he had brushed my teeth for me when I'd been semi-helpless in a boot and a pair of crutches. Then I spotted the scar on his left arm, where a bullet had pierced his skin when he had been trying to help me get away from the men who wanted to kill me. Even now, I could reflect on how cavalier he had been about the whole thing. What had he said?

"Just a flesh wound," Seth murmured, unraveling a roll of gauze in his hands.

Suddenly, every hair stood up on the back of my neck as I looked at Seth, really taking the man in for the first time. Without judgment. Without resentment. Without fear.

It was him.

It had to be him.

The scar on his arm from the bullet hole should have been enough to prove his true identity all along. But I had been too stubborn and resilient to believe it, fighting and scratching with all my might to push him away. So I sat there and watched him wrap the fresh wound on my leg with bandages, meticulous as ever. My breathing increased, because I knew in my heart that everything he had confessed to me on Sunday night was real.

"How does that feel?" Seth secured the gauze just above my ankle, where his hand remained. I felt my body awakening at his touch and knew that I didn't want him to stop.

"Good," I whispered, blushing subtle pink. "Better."

Seth caught my eye, his crystal blue gems diminishing into thin rings, overpowered by the dominating blacks of his pupils. Not a word was spoken. But in that moment, I think he knew. Because I had no way of convincing him otherwise.

He realized that I had believed him implicitly, which meant that there was hope for us after all. That we were no longer doomed. A sliver of light had burst forth into a promising beacon of all that was to come. Of a future that aligned more closely with the past.

"I'm sorry about what I said," Seth admitted, his eyes still and unblinking.

"I'm sorry too." I pressed my lips together and smiled, communicating with my eyes what I had never been able to with my mouth. Cabel had always been better at body language, but that didn't mean I couldn't find other ways to get what I wanted.

My voice turned soft and silky, the closest I had ever come to imitating velvet. Even if he said no, I could persuade him with the luxurious decadence of my words. It wasn't what I said—no, that was never the trick. It was the way I said it.

"Can you make sure I don't have any scratches anywhere else?" I gently crooned, maintaining a loose sense of balance as I slumped forward, tempting his willpower.

Seth said nothing. But his alluring eyes sized me up, drifting from head to toe and all the places in between, while I waited for him to search me. His hand ghosted over the bandages around the bottom of my leg. As his hypnotic gaze stayed on mine, his palm drifted from my ankle to my calf to my thigh. He inched close enough to stand between my legs and I swallowed, his mere presence stopping my heart in a second.

When he leaned in, my pulse quickened. I felt his breath on my lips and tensed with anticipation for all that he had done and all that he had yet to do. But the act was merely a tease, as he stuck his head over my shoulder to look down at my back.

"No scratches here," he whispered, resting his hands along either side of my arms.

I angled my face towards his and looked on with the curiosity of a feral cat. As his eyes flitted over my rosy features, I licked my lips and grasped the edge of the countertop for support. I may have been sitting down, but I was growing weaker and weaker in the knees. With every passing second, I didn't know how to endure even an inch of distance.

"No scratches here either." Seth touched my shoulders and then set his fingers against my neck. Awakening parts of my soul that I had buried for months, he traced a line from the bottom of my throat to the top of my sternum. My eyes slightly widened to meet his, as he opened his palm over my chest, feeling the rapid heart beating beneath it.

I sank my teeth into my lower lip and sucked a deep breath of air into my lungs, somewhat nervous that he knew exactly how he affected me. But when his hand curved along my waist and around the back of my ribcage, I didn't stop him. Whether Seth knew it or not, he was free to touch whatever part of me he wanted. It was all his anyway.

When he bowed his head and placed a delicate kiss over my shoulder, I tilted my head back and sighed. My eyelids slid shut with the reassuring caress, and I hoped he had more planned for me than the softest touch of his lips. He kneaded the flesh above my hips with his hands, grabbing and stretching and tugging. I inhaled at the pressure and wanted more.

Reading my mind, Seth blazed a trail from one side of my clavicle to the other with his mouth, his thumb digging into the dip at the base of my throat. I whimpered at the sensation and threaded my fingers through his blonde locks, pulling and jerking. The force elicited a deep growl from the back of his throat, and I felt my insides melting at the sound. As his hands traveled up and down my bare back, I slipped under his spell.

"You're so beautiful," he sighed, gazing deep into my eyes.

I held my breath, nearly going numb at the way he sent tingles along the surface of my skin, making me shiver and burn all at the same time. When he touched his lips to my neck, I was pulsing with that warm, aching need, a yearning desire to be his again. He swept my hair over my shoulders and ran his hands down the length of my arms, all the while planting sweet kisses wherever his mouth decided to roam.

Caught up in the moment, I forgot everything that had happened over the past few months. The fear. The lie. The baby. For a split second, I glimpsed a spark of flashing light in his ice blue eyes and knew that he could heal me in places that no one else could. Only he alone could glue the shattered pieces of my heart back together again.

His teeth skimmed over the edge of my earlobe, while I dug my nails into the nape of his neck and cried out with pleasure. Then his fingertips sank into the small of my back, and I brushed my lips over his jawline, begging and coaxing. He squeezed my warm flesh in his hands, calming and searing every part of me all at once. It was like fire and ice, the way I felt so suddenly flustered with heat, while simultaneous shivers crept down my spine.

Breathless, I cupped his cheek in my hand and felt his strong jawline underneath. "Make love to me," I murmured, my fingers dancing over the stubble on his face.

He held his chin up and swallowed, gazing down at me with uncertainty. When a crinkle formed between his blonde brows, I slid the pad of my thumb over the line. Surprised, he clamped his hand around my wrist and then kissed the innermost part of my palm, where I already had a throbbing pulse. I flitted my eyes up to meet his and bit my lower lip again, sinking my teeth in deeper this time, no matter the discomfort.

Alive with passion, he scooped me up in his arms and carried me into the bedroom. My body was on fire, his hands scorching me in every place he touched. When he laid me down on the mattress, the back of my head was cradled against the pillow, but all I wanted was his warm, strong body on top of mine. Where it was meant to be.

Impatient, I rocked forward onto my knees and wrapped my hands around the back of his neck, fixing my lips on his and consuming his mouth until he could hardly breathe. He groaned when I scraped my fingernails across his shoulder blades, feeling the hard, sinewy muscle there. When the space between us dissolved, our torsos became flush and I couldn't handle the feel of his bare stomach against mine. It was so much, yet not enough.

I rested my elbows on his back, and he pulled me into his lap. My knees sat along either side of his hips, as I fell into another kiss, crushing his lips to mine. The way our mouths were working against each other's reminded me of how things used to be, and I knew now more than ever that I would do whatever it took to get that feeling back again.

"I love you," he rasped against my mouth, inhaling air between kisses. "I'll always love you." His hand slithered down my spine, and I could hardly handle what he was doing to my body and mind. I was melting from his words, shivering from his touch.

"Show me," I pleaded, holding his head up so he was forced to look into my eyes. "Show me how much you love me."

He took a swift breath and molded his mouth to mine, sandwiching my bottom lip between his teeth. A whimper escaped me as his fingers weaved through my hair, twisting and tangling until my dark tresses felt like they were in knots. He grabbed my hip and dragged me across the bed, leaning down over my willing body as our lips met again and again. With a hammering pulse in my ears, I coiled my arms around his back and hugged him tight. There had never been a stronger shelter than the one I found in his embrace.

My head lolled back as his lips returned to my sternum, his hands skating over my spine. I brought my mouth to his and hummed, while he rested his forehead against mine and opened his eyes. In that brief silence, I rubbed my cheek against his and sighed.

Then his fingers crept close enough to reach my bikini top, and he untied the strings.

Chapter 36

Curling into Seth's chest, I stretched out and felt the salty sweat that remained on my skin. My lips left a string of kisses along his torso, as he kept his arm around my back, securely holding my body in place. Though my heart rate had yet to rest, I felt an underlying sense of peace and calm, nestled in his tender strength.

With a sigh of contentment, Seth lifted my chin in his hand and gazed down at my face, stroking the edge of my jawline. Swallowing, I caught my breath and leaned forward to gift a soft kiss on his lips. They were as full and lush as I had remembered, during a time when the taste of his mouth had been a cardinal sin, and I was his Achilles heel. He brushed the hair out of my face and kissed my temple, his fingers trailing my spine.

"How do you feel?" Seth wondered, his eyes light blue and scorching bright.

"Good," I murmured, my cheeks staining with blush at the confession.

He brushed his thumb along either of my lips, unable to hide a complacent grin. Regarding the smug smirk willfully, I kept my eyes on his and turned to putty in his hands. Seth swept his fingers across my shoulder and I shuddered, reacting to his electric touch on demand. Even now, I was lost in the afterglow and trembling.

But then the levy broke, because my heart was exposed. In that one encounter, I had bared my soul to Seth and succumbed to whoever he was. I had loved him before, and I could love him again. Mostly because I had never stopped. Despite every attempt to lengthen the discord between us, one truth remained. I was in love with him.

"Finley," he called, tucking a lock of hair behind my ear. "Are you okay?"

As tears pooled in my eyes, Seth sat up in the bed, his demeanor shaping into one laced with fear and worry. But I wasn't crying because I was sad. Heavy teardrops were skirting down my face because of the way he had made me feel. The emotion was overwhelming, because I had never been left feeling so complete. I felt whole again, like the damage between us had been undone. It wasn't perfect, but it was a start.

"Yeah," I cooed, keeping my head down to mask the sensation. "I'm fine."

But Seth knew me too well, cradling my limp body against his side as we lay wrapped in the sheets. He dried my eyes and kissed the top of my head, consoling me with delicate care, like I was his little girl. "What's on your mind?" he posed, clever and sharp.

Swallowing, I flicked my eyes up to meet Seth's

and became a decent representation of a weeping willow. The tension between us had never been about his identity. Deep down, I didn't care whether his name was Cabel or Seth. I loved my husband, whoever he was.

"I wanted to have a child," I croaked. "Your child."

Seth took my face in his hands and exhaled, his blue eyes desperately searching mine.

"And what if I can never—"

"Stop," Seth interrupted. "Don't say that. Don't do this to yourself."

I sniffled and sobbed, re-breaking all of the places that he had just mended. What if I couldn't be healed? Emotionally, he was piecing me back together again. But physically. My body would do what it wanted, because biology was something that neither of us could control. If that were the case, the worry and distress would surely do me in.

"I know how much you wanted this baby," I explained. "I wanted her, too."

"I know you did, Finley. But you're still young. And we can try again."

Those words terrified me, because I was so scared of disappointment. I had never planned for Cayley to come into my life when she did. But now that she was gone, I couldn't imagine never having so much love growing inside me again.

My mind was jumping ahead, momentarily diverted like skipping stones over a pond. Despite the internal war I had waged against myself, I felt guilty for having a miscarriage. While I didn't blame him anymore for being unable to spare me the pain, I worried that I wouldn't be able to provide what he had always wanted. A family of his own.

Seth was a good-looking man, well-employed, not quite thirty. How could I let him waste a lifetime with me if children were something that I could never supply him with? The slight possibility of not being able to fulfill my purpose as a woman felt like an ice cold bucket of water on my soul. What if Cayley had been my only chance? Was that it?

"No, Finley. Don't," he begged, staring into my eyes with such longing and affection, such unconditional love, that the way I felt nearly ripped my heart in two.

"I can't help it." I shook my head and turned away, covering my face with my hands. I was ashamed and horrified, truly losing faith in what we had. I wanted to believe that our misfortunes were over, that we wouldn't have to keep living with the pain. I was wrong.

Without a word, Seth grabbed my elbow and planted his mouth on mine, kissing and loving and coaxing. I whimpered at the sudden contact until he silenced me with his lips. Those strong fingertips of his dug into my arms, but I couldn't resist the pleasurable warmth that pulsed through my body when he held me like that.

I hummed when he claimed my mouth, falling

prey to whatever he had in store. As his hands traveled up and down my back, I felt my insides unfurling at the delicate touch and pushed all worries about pregnancy out of my mind for now. Seth rose up on his knees and lowered my body to the mattress, hovering above me as he kissed me with everything he had. I could hardly breathe when his bare torso pressed against mine, his hands smoothing along the inner part of my arms, while every inch of my skin did nothing but sing.

When his lips landed on my throat, I let my head sink into the pillow and relaxed beneath him. Seth folded his fingers through mine and burrowed our hands into the mattress, his urgent mouth returning to mine faster than I could blink. I wanted to breathe and share his air, drawing the power of his oxygen into my lungs. It gave me strength, because I knew now that I would never leave. I didn't want to. Unless he made me.

Seductively whispering my name, Seth captured my mouth and groaned in a way that made my insides tingle all over again. Desperate for him, I wiggled my hands free from his grasp and pierced my fingernails into his back. Seth stilled above me and gasped, his sweet breath raining down on my face, like a warm veil of comfort in the night.

His love was divine and pure.

I wanted to drown in it.

Chapter 37

For the remainder of the trip, Seth and I were inseparable. In many ways, everything between us had stayed the same. I loved my golden boy. My beautiful man. My faithful husband. He was the only one to ever claim my heart. The only one I loved.

Our time in the mountains felt like a dream. But the fairytale mood dissolved when the week-long vacation reached an end. The night before we had to leave, Seth turned quiet and morose. As we soaked in the bathtub together, I worried that there were more secrets and lies he had yet to share with me. If I had fallen for another ruse, I wouldn't be able to forgive him this time.

"Seth?" I looked over my shoulder at him, trying to ignore the fact that it felt like saying a stranger's name. There was a stigma there, because I was so used to Cabel.

He sat behind me with his head ducked down, his elbows resting against his knees. There was something sad that had taken his alluring features and diminished their light. That furrowed brow. Those crystal eyes murky and downcast. I would have given anything to know what was going on in that head of his.

He failed to answer me, so I scooped a puff of white foam in my hand and blew it at him. Only a real man would take a bubble bath with his wife, and that's what he was. But when he chuckled and batted the dollop of suds away, a brief smile quickly flitted across his face. Before I could commit the sweet expression to memory, it was gone.

"Hey," I whispered, cuddling up close to him in the tub. "What's wrong?"

He placed his hand at the top of my back, but the gesture felt forced. "Nothing."

Narrowing my eyes at him, I turned his chin to the side with my hand and kissed his neck. Seth stiffened at my touch, but then his fingers were stroking my back as he molded his lips to mine, pulling me in. I welcomed the sensual affection and ignored any signs that something could be wrong, because I hated to admit that something always was.

In bed that night, I lay there with my head on Seth's chest, warm and content. My mind flashed through images of the past week and our time together. Despite everything that had happened, including his big fat lie, I truly felt happy again. We could rebuild whatever bridges had been burned, because they would ultimately lead us back to each other.

But as I lifted my head to gaze up at Seth in the

dark, I failed to find a similar sense of hopefulness flitting across his features. Seth looked stern, sullen, and upset. His jaw was clenched and his eyes were on the ceiling, while I wondered what could have him feeling so low.

Not wanting to pry, I resumed my previous posture and shut my eyes. No matter what tomorrow had in store for us, I knew that we would be able to handle it. Together. So I cast every possible worry aside and drifted off in his arms.

* * *

On Saturday morning, I woke up to the sound of zippers shutting and doors closing. Struggling to open my eyes, I noticed the empty side of the bed to my right and frowned. Sun beamed in through the window, and I tossed the covers over my head.

By the time I made it downstairs, there was a plate of bacon and eggs waiting for me, as well as a single glass of orange juice. I pulled a wooden stool out and sat down at the bar in front of the kitchen. I hadn't seen Seth though I had heard him earlier, but I was too hungry to wait until he arrived.

So I scarfed down my breakfast and washed the dishes in the sink. When I finished, Seth trudged in and plopped down on the couch. The fact that he hadn't even acknowledged my presence made my eye twitch. I had that feeling again—the one that told me not to trust. It left knots in my stomach and a lump in my throat. But I pushed forward and joined him in the living room anyway.

"Good morning," I chirped, feeling lively and energetic from the home cooked meal. "Thanks for making me breakfast."

"It was no problem." Seth stared at the empty fireplace and slouched between the couch cushions. He hadn't made eye contact.

"Did you sleep well?" I probed. If he had lain awake all night staring at the ceiling overhead, then I could understand why he was acting like a zombie. But if he hadn't...

"Yeah," he mouthed, sitting there like the most lifeless human being on earth.

Nervous, I took a seat on the arm of the couch that was closest to me and tried not to panic. He probably had a lot on his mind. He probably had to start planning for the rest of the semester. He was probably just tired. Those were the things I had to tell myself, hypothesizing the possible reasons for his behavior that had no influence of mine.

"Seth, you need to talk to me," I insisted.

His eyes met mine for just a moment, and I hated feeling like he was hiding something. While he had kept dangerous secrets from me before, I didn't want to feel like I couldn't trust him. If he could be truly honest with me, that was worth more than anything else.

"Why?" He kept his head down and rubbed

his palms together. "What's the point?"

I rose from the couch and stood before him, so entirely caught off guard. We made a vow. He had given me a ring. Didn't that mean anything to him?

"What's going on?" I questioned, not liking the way my body was already reacting to the stress.

"I just think it would be easier for both of us if we weren't on speaking terms."

"Excuse me?" I snapped, immediately raising my voice. "What are you talking about?"

He closed his eyes and took a deep breath. Then he opened them and said, "You have to understand how hard this is for me."

I took a step back and swallowed.

"But we made a deal," he noted. "And I have to let you go."

Paralyzed and stunned, I remained stock still with my hands at my sides. He didn't want me. He didn't love me. Not anymore.

Tears welled up in my eyes, as I looked at him and cried. "You once said that you would never let me go," I reminded him. "What happened to that man?"

Seth's head popped up. For the first time today, he looked truly worried, concerned that he had hurt me. I didn't know if I was sad or angry. It felt like a combination of both.

He knitted his eyebrows together and announced, "I don't want to let you go. But I know that I've made you unhappy."

I felt the painful lump in my throat and sobbed.

"You deserve a chance at a life without me. I don't want to hurt you anymore." Seth glanced up at me with watery eyes. "I understand why you decided—"

"Decided what?" I cried.

He set his hand over his thigh and looked utterly confused. "We've been here a whole week, and you haven't said anything. I thought—"

"So you just assumed?" I swiped my tears away as they stung.

"Finley, I just want to do what's best for you. I'll do whatever you want."

Fuming over his stupidity, I squatted down before him and grasped his face in my hands. "I don't want a divorce."

He blinked a few times, stunned. "You don't?"

I shook my head and whispered, "Not now. Not ever."

"Really?" he mouthed, making sure.

"Yes," I hissed, letting the tears run down my face. I had lost my husband before. I wasn't losing him again.

Relief washed over Seth as he gathered me in his arms and squeezed tight. My knees dug into the floor, though I kept him wrapped in my embrace. He had scared me to death, but my heart rate was stabilizing. Like always, everything had been one big misunderstanding.

"I'm sorry," he crooned, his hand in my hair.

"I'm so sorry."

Just as relieved as he was, I let the calm flood through me and inhaled. Seth picked my body up off the floor and placed me in his lap, where I remained with my head on his shoulder for the next hour. If we had any more miscommunications, I didn't know if my spirit would be able to handle it.

"I'm sorry about the baby," he eventually said.

"It's not your fault," I accepted. "None of it is."

"Finley."

"I forgive you." My arm was curled around his neck as I placed an innocent kiss on his cheek. "For all of it."

He touched the side of my face with the palm of his hand and looked into my eyes. "I'd understand if you didn't want to."

"But I do." I rubbed my nose against his throat and leaned in for a kiss.

"I want you to call me Cabel," he said before our lips met.

"What?" I didn't understand. "But—"

"That's my name now. It has been for a while." His breath rushed over my mouth as he confessed, "I've missed hearing you say it."

A newly formed tear glided down my cheek as I smiled. If I could start calling him by that familiar name like I used to, every shattered piece would have fallen into place. My heart was back together again.

"I've missed saying it."

He wiped the lonely teardrop away and threaded his fingers through my hair.

"You'll always be Cabel Jones to me."

He unleashed a crooked grin that had gone into hiding and sealed the truth with a kiss.

Chapter 38

In order to ease back into my old life, I started waiting tables at the restaurant three nights a week. Jeremy was glad to have me back and even let me train the new girl who had just started that week. When he caught me teaching her how to keep from dropping serving trays and knocking drinks over on the table, Jeremy's green eyes lit up with delight and he winked. We had all been there. Surely, he remembered when I had.

With the semester nearly over, I registered for summer classes so I could pick up where I had left off. Somehow, realizing that my grad school dreams hadn't been squashed meant the world to me. Despite everything that had happened in the past, life could go on.

I believed that now.

One sunny day when Cabel was done putting in final grades for the semester, I found him sorting through papers in his office at home. His desk was always so organized that I couldn't believe he had left it unattended for this long, even though the last week had been so hectic. I opened the French doors and surprised him, waltzing towards him in a new pink dress.

"Hey, baby," he chimed, looking me up and down. "You must be in a good mood today."

I strolled towards him without a word and placed a light kiss on his mouth. When he hummed in response, I sat down in his lap and circled my arms around the nape of his neck. Beaming, Cabel placed his arm over my back and leaned forward in the chair.

"I'm almost done here," he said, reluctant to have work priorities to attend to.

"That's okay. I'll wait." I wanted his undivided attention. Closing my eyes, I wrapped my arms around Cabel's torso and rested my head on his chest as he worked. "Am I clingy?" I wondered.

"You?"

I looked up at him and admired the sarcastic grin. It was hilarious and beautiful all at once.

"Yes," he admitted. "But I like clingy."

"Good." I opened the top of his shirt and kissed his sternum. I wanted his skin all over mine. Especially now.

Respectful of his commitment to the job, I waited patiently until he was finished with all of his duties as a professor. Sometimes I thought back to moments in my life with Cabel. The day we met. The first time he kissed me. The night I told him that I was in love with him. And the moment that he revealed the same. Every day with him was a blessing, and I didn't want my life any other way.

"All done," Cabel announced, tossing his ink

pen aside.

My eyes lifted to his with a devilish smirk as he leaned forward to claim my mouth. We crashed into each other, needing and grabbing and wanting. When his fingers crawled up my leg, I held him tighter and groaned.

In an instant, Cabel stood with me in his arms and dashed out of the room. My legs folded around his waist as he climbed up the staircase and brought me into the bedroom. I twisted my fingers through his hair and made sure that his lips never left mine.

He reached the bed and stepped out of his shoes before climbing on top of me. Frantically fiddling with the buttons on his shirt, I managed to take the garment off and toss it across the room before either of us spontaneously combusted. Cabel shed the rest of his clothes and then smoothed his hand along the top of my thigh so he could peel off the dress.

"I thought we were going out to dinner," I gasped against his mouth, feeling his hand settle along my waistline.

He moaned and then suggested, "Let's stay in tonight."

His lips grazed over my earlobe and I uttered, "Okay," shamelessly succumbing.

* * *

It was dark outside by the time I realized how hungry I was. Cabel lay in bed beside me, his thumb circling over the edge of my shoulder. He had already caught his breath and was smiling, so it seemed like the right moment. Surely better planned than last time.

I pressed my cheek into the cool pillow and said, "I'm pregnant."

Cabel chuckled. "I'm pretty sure it takes a little longer than that." When the glowing expression left my face, he sat up on his elbows and looked at me, as if for the first time. "Really?"

"I took a pregnancy test, and I've already been to the doctor."

His mouth dropped wide open, and I loved that I had been able to surprise him. It was supposed to feel like this. Like the whole world came to a screeching halt for the two of us.

"Why didn't you tell me?" he probed.

"I wanted to be sure," I admitted.

"Are you?"

I smiled so wide that it nearly busted my cheeks. "Yes."

He chewed the edge of his lip with a grin. "We're going to have a baby?"

"Yes," I whispered, nearly at the point of tears. "Yes. We are."

Cabel hugged me close as we held each other tight. I loved being wrapped in his arms, knowing that his child was already growing inside me. He kissed my hair, and he kissed my face, radiating joy. I could truly tell how happy he was, and that meant everything to me.

We talked for a while, his voice soft enough to lull anyone to sleep. As I lay there in the night, he clung to my frame and placed his hand over my stomach. Then he rested his head on my chest, and everything was as I had always imagined it to be.

Chapter 39

When the day finally arrived for our sweet little girl to enter this world, I found myself writhing in pain at the hospital. I screamed and cursed, digging my nails into Cabel's palm and nearly breaking his arm off. But in the end, it was all worth it.

Elusive baby Cayley was here at last.

"She looks just like her father," I told the nurse. But she didn't seem too concerned about it.

"It's not uncommon," she explained, checking my vitals with a blood pressure cuff. "Her looks will change as she gets older."

I rolled my head to the side and tried to relax when she was done. But I had just had a baby, and I was in a rush to get out of this uncomfortable bed. The stale smell of plastic and hand sanitizer was starting to burn my nose. I was ready to go home.

"Where is he anyway?" I asked, grouchy. "My husband, I mean."

The nurse looked over her shoulder and smiled, retrieving her clipboard. "Looks like he left you for another woman."

At that very moment, Cabel walked in with our daughter comfortably cradled in his arms. The nurse who had accompanied him back from the other wing of the hospital made sure that I was feeling well before leaving the three of us alone together. I watched as she disappeared into the hallway and appreciated the fact that she shut the door behind her.

"Well," Cabel began, sitting down on the edge of my cot. "Her lungs are clear and she's had all her shots. I'd say she's healthy as a horse."

I looked on at the sleeping beauty in his arms, unable to believe that we had made her. She was mine. She was his. She was ours. Nothing felt more right.

"Let me hold her," I demanded, missing my little girl already.

Cabel was careful setting her in my arms as her eyelids fluttered back and forth. I hoped that she was dreaming of oceans and unicorns and castles in the sky. The feel of her small head against my heart made it beat quicker, and I was in love. Forever. Always.

"She's beautiful," Cabel observed, looking over us with tender affection.

"That's because she looks just like you." I bobbed my head at him and smirked.

"She looks like you, too," he insisted. "You just can't see it yet. One day you will though."

"I won't hold my breath on that one," I sarcastically replied.

My attention returned to Cayley, as I let her hold my pinkie in her hand. Her fingernails were so tiny, almost too precious to be real. I could hardly believe it.

Cabel and I went on talking quietly as I held her in my tired arms. Then the most amazing thing happened. Sweet baby Cayley opened her eyes, but just for a moment. We held each other's gaze, and though she couldn't speak, I felt her tiny spirit drifting through me. She was an infant magician and sorceress who already had me under her spell.

Cayley stared into my eyes as I whispered sweet words to her. The sight of her looking up at me was so emotional that tears welled up in my eyes. Because I remembered all that her father and I had gone through to get here, to this very moment in time, with her in my arms. But then she fell back asleep and I laughed, sniffling all the while.

When I glanced over at Cabel, he was staring at the two of us. The gentle, kind, caring man that he was, my husband wiped my tears away. Then he planted a kiss on my forehead and did the same to Cayley. These were the two loves of my life. My husband and our beautiful new member of the Jones family. The one I had been waiting for all along. The one who had never let me give up hope. The one who had finally made it.

Our daughter. Little Miss Cayley Jones.

Chapter 40

When Cayley was three months old, I stirred awake one night to the sound of her crying. The space beside me in bed was still warm, yet empty. My body felt broken, exhausted from a lack of sleep and a surplus of breastfeeding.

But I stumbled out of bed anyway and slipped my robe on. By the time I reached the hallway, Cayley had stopped crying and I felt relieved. With a hand through my tangled locks, I crept towards the nursery and stuck my head in the open doorway.

Cabel stood in front of the crib with Cayley in his arms, gently swaying from side to side. He rubbed her back, and I listened as she cooed, easily drifting back into a deep sleep. Laying her down in her crib, Cabel made sure she was flat on her back before he leaned over her and left a tender kiss on her forehead, thinking there was no one but the two of them in the room.

When Cabel turned on his heel and discovered that I had been watching, I didn't mind being caught. I had snuck up on him at the best possible time, because those fleeting moments he spent with our daughter are the stuff life is made of.

Coming towards me, Cabel grabbed my hand, pulled the door to, and then led me back down the hallway. Before we reached our room, I stopped him and wrapped my hands around the top of his arms. "You're a good man," I murmured.

Cabel looked down at me and smiled. "All I know is that I love you. And I love our little girl in there."

Filled with warmth, I leaned up on the tips of my toes and claimed his mouth. It took Cabel by surprise but I liked that.

"Does this mean you're ready to make another one, Mrs. Jones?" he asked.

"I don't know." I let go of him and walked into the bedroom. "Maybe."

Cabel chased after me and grabbed ahold of my wrist, twirling me back into his arms. "Miss O'Connell," he scolded, squeezing my sides. "Where do you think you're going?"

I leaned into his body and kept his eyes on mine. "Wherever you are."

Cabel lifted his hand to my face and dragged his thumb along my cheekbone.

I sighed and pressed my cheek into his palm, gazing into the eyes of my one true love. My first love. My last love. The love that creates new love and bleeds out pain.

Love that comes once in a lifetime. Love that

stands the test of time.

As Cabel and I curled up together in the night, he draped his arm across my torso in a protective manner and kissed my hair. When he fell asleep and I could hear him breathing, it became clear to me that of all the many loves a person can have over the course of a lifetime, Cabel was all of mine.

Tell Me Your Favorite Part!

If you enjoyed Mr. Jones & Me, I invite you to head over to Amazon and let me know your favorite part. Reviews are so important to an author's career, because they help new readers like you discover the book. Even if you didn't enjoy Mr. Jones & Me, I'd still love it if you could take three minutes to let me know what you think of the book.

Leaving a review is super easy:

1) Go to Mr. Jones & Me Book Page on Amazon

2) Scroll Down and click "Write a Customer Review"

3) Sign in to Amazon if prompted

4) Select a star rating

5) Write a few short words (or long words, I won't judge)

6) Click the 'submit' button

I thank you in advance!

Acknowledgements

Thank you to my loving mother and father. You guys are my support system, my best friends, my #1 fans. The late night talks and pats on the back mean more than you will ever know.

To my remaining family and close friends, thank you for cheering me on at every turn. Life can be scary sometimes, but with all of you around, I know I can always take the good with the bad and smile.

Many thanks to all who participated in the release of *S.I.N.G.L.E.*! Special thanks to *Give Me Books* for hosting the Cover Reveal & Release Blitz as well as all bloggers/reviewers who signed up. Also, thank you to Larissa at *The Howling Turtle*, Naylene at *More than Scribbles*, Kathleen at *Celtic Lady's Reviews*, Yvonne at *Socrates' Book Reviews*, Mandy at *I Read Indie*, Kristy at *Keep Calm and Write On*, Dani at *Paulette's Papers*, Nina at *Life of a Bookworm*, Lisa at *Lisa Loves Literature*, Leisha O. at *Rolo Polo Book Blog*, Amber at *Sapphyria's Book Reviews*, *Nerd Girl Official*, *Reading Between the Wines Book Club*,

Jessica Hernandez, Amanda Leigh, Mercedes Fox, Dante Craddock, Monique McDonell, Jennifer Levac, Mrs. Mommy Booknerd, LT Kelly, and Micalea Smeltzer.

Also, to any other authors, bloggers, reviewers that I may have missed. Thank you so much for everything. You all are the backbone of my journey as a writer.

And finally, to my loyal readers and fans. Thank you so much for taking the time to read my books and tell your friends and leave reviews. All of you are amazing, and I'm so glad to finally give you the follow up to Finley and Cabel's story that so many of you have been asking for. Henry and Elaine are next in line, with Addie and Tom right behind them. But I might have a few tricks up my sleeve before then. So you'll just have to wait and see...

I love you all so much and hope you know that I'm giving each of you a very big hug right now :)

About the Author

Lindsay Marie Miller was born and raised in Tallahassee, Florida, where she graduated from high school as Valedictorian. At sixteen, she started writing her first novel, *Emerald Green*, after being inspired by Stephenie Meyer's International Bestselling *Twilight Saga*. During her time in college, Lindsay wrote 5 more novels and over 100 songs. After graduating Summa Cum Laude from Florida State University, she put her B.A. in English Literature to good use and published her debut novel, *Emerald Green*. An author of over 10 Romance Titles, Lindsay currently resides in her hometown of Tallahassee where she is always working on her next novel.

To learn more, please visit:

www.lindsaymariemillerauthor.com

Sign up for Lindsay's newsletter:

lindsaymariemillerauthor.com/claim-your-free-book/

Join Lindsay on Facebook at:

facebook.com/LindsayMarieMillerAuthor

Follow Lindsay on Twitter at:

twitter.com/Lindsay_MMiller

www.ingramcontent.com/pod-product-compliance
Lightning Source LLC
Chambersburg PA
CBHW030027180626
46810CB00001B/251